The noises of stream and woodland faded. Leigh was helpless to do anything but return the kiss in full measure. Feeling her response, Morgan's arms tensed, then he released her hands, one arm sliding down to gather her closer, the other hand gliding up beneath her hair to frame her head and deny her the right to refuse the deep, sensual demand of his kiss.

Leigh's mind was totally shattered by the revelation of that embrace. When Morgan tore his mouth away from hers, she could only stare up at him dazedly from beneath heavy lids. But even as she watched, she saw horror and disgust sweep all signs of passion from his face.

'No!' He thrust her away so hard she almost fell. 'No, by God, not me! I loathe and despise all that you and your mother stand for. I won't be another scalp on your belts. One fool in this family is enough! I'd have to be really desperate to accept what you're offering, Leigh. Save it for some other poor fool.'

SOMETHING FROM THE HEART

BY
AMANDA BROWNING

MILLS & BOON LIMITED
ETON HOUSE   18-24 PARADISE ROAD
RICHMOND   SURREY   TW9 1SR

*First published in Great Britain 1990
by Mills & Boon Limited*

© Amanda Browning 1990

*Australian copyright 1990
Philippine copyright 1991
This edition 1991*

ISBN 0 263 76918 6

*Set in Times Roman 10 on 10¼ pt.
01-9101-62057 C*

Made and printed in Great Britain

CHAPTER ONE

'MORGAN'S coming home.'

Those three words her stepfather uttered so joyfully over the breakfast table gave Leigh Armstrong's nerves an almighty jolt, and sent her heart sinking somewhere south of her knees, from where it only slowly began to rise again. The slice of toast she had been eating fell forgotten on to her plate as she glanced across at Ralph Fairfax. His pleasure at his only son's imminent return was obvious. Because he had been more than just a father to her all these years, had been her friend too, and because she loved him, she couldn't let him see that her joy was definitely mixed.

She was out of her seat in an instant, going to slip her arms about Ralph's shoulders and press a kiss to his craggy cheek. She was happy for him, she really was. She only wished she could have been as happy for herself. A year ago she would have had no misgivings, but things had changed between herself and her stepbrother Morgan. None of which was Ralph's fault, and she wasn't about to burden him with her problems.

'When is he coming?' she asked, glad to hear her enthusiasm didn't sound too forced.

Ralph gave a self-conscious laugh. 'I forgot to read that part. Here,' he thrust the paper at her, 'you look.'

She took it with a shake of her head, dropping another kiss on to the top of his head before returning to her own seat. 'The most important bit and you miss it!' she teased. Her heart beat a little faster as she ran her eyes over Morgan's forceful black script. It seemed as uncompromising as she remembered him last, and she had to repress a tiny shiver. 'He says here "I'll be over on the twenty-second." When is that?' She did a rapid mental calculation, and her heart sank. 'Why, that's next week.' Too soon. Much too soon. Like a jack-in-the-box, she was on her feet again. 'I'd better tell Rose. She'll need to know. Then I'll make a start on his room. We never did get around to spring-cleaning it.' Because she had kept putting it off.

'Aren't you going to finish your breakfast first?' Ralph called after her in mild surprise as she made for the door.

Leigh paused in the doorway. 'Who could eat at a time like this? It isn't every day we hear that Morgan's coming home.' She grinned, turning it into a joke, but the truth was her stomach was in no state to accept food right now. To her relief, Ralph laughed too.

'You're right. I was forgetting about that special bond you two share. I remember now it was always the same whenever Morgan was due home from school. You wouldn't eat, and then you dogged his footsteps like Peter Pan's shadow. His patience must have been phenomenal. The things you'd get up to would make a saint wince! Still, it's my belief Morgan would forgive you anything,' Ralph reminisced affectionately.

Colour flooded her cheeks. She had thought so too, but their last meeting had rocked her out of her complacency. 'You make me sound like an unholy terror. I'm sure I was never that bad.'

'If anything, you were worse!' he retorted, smiling. 'But it only added to your charm. Well, run along if you must, but I'll expect you to eat all your lunch.'

A genuine smile blossomed at that stricture. 'Yes, Ralph,' she agreed demurely, and hurried away to the sound of his laughter.

Rose, their housekeeper, accepted the good news with plans to get in a store of Morgan's favourite foods. Leigh left her still chattering to herself and took the back stairs with a wry smile on her face. It was as if she had uttered a magic word. Substitute Morgan for abracadabra. It should have released a flood of warm memories for herself, too, but instead there was only that last one, blotting the rest out.

Outside his room, she hesitated. Another first. Usually she would have walked straight in, but she had been avoiding doing that assiduously for months because she knew how strong his presence was inside. Going in would be like facing him again, so grim-faced and distant, hearing him say those things that were so unlike him. Yet it had to be faced, and it would be better to get it over with before he arrived. Taking a deep breath, she quickly slipped inside, closing the door and leaning back against it.

Done out in autumn shades, it was a very masculine room. She had been in it countless times over the years since her mother had married Morgan's father. There were cups and medals on the shelves, trophies of his school years, and she had laboured hard over polishing them, basking in the reflected glory of knowing they belonged to her brother. She had always been welcome, and allowed to use the room as a sanctuary when her mother made life unbearable. Now, though, she felt like an intruder, and all because of a terrible misunderstanding.

Even now she found it hard to believe that one incident could change their relationship so drastically. Morgan had been so kind to her when, willing or not, he had acquired her as a new stepsister. She had been ten to his eighteen. A very wary ten-year-old. Una Armstrong's marriage to Ralph Fairfax had been the latest in a long line into which she had dragged her small daughter. By then, Leigh had had few illusions left about her mother, realising that any love Una possessed was for herself. The term amoral wouldn't have meant anything to Leigh then, but she had known she didn't like the way her mother lived her life. She had longed for a real family, and when each marriage had failed to produce it she had adopted a defensive layer in order to survive the loneliness.

Then Una had married Ralph, a kind, gentle man who had opened his generous heart to her. But it had taken Morgan's acceptance to convince her that this time it was going to be different. At eighteen, on the verge of going to university, he had been a youthful version of the man he was to become—tall, dark, with an athlete's leanly powerful body, blue-eyed and ruggedly handsome. When they met, she had seen the pity in his eyes for his father, and the total contempt for her mother, but when he had looked at her he had smiled, and the world had seemed to take on a glow as she tentatively returned that offering.

It had been the beginning of a whole new life for Leigh—filled with warmth and laughter that had helped her blossom into the full potential of her nature. There had been no looking back, even when Ralph's disillusionment with his marriage was at its worst. She had never been happier. Morgan treated her to the offhand affection of an older brother, never seeming to mind that if he turned around he would most likely trip over her. He was the recipient of her childhood confidences, and seemed possessed of an endless patient amusement.

After university, where Morgan had studied architecture, he had gone to America for five years and they had seen very little of him. It had been Leigh's turn to be at university when he finally returned, yet it was as if nothing had changed. They had still shared the same camaraderie whenever they met. However, the intervals had grown longer as Morgan set up his own business and took projects abroad. Leigh had studied hard and gained a history degree—and in a flash, another two years had gone by.

With an odd little sigh, Leigh crossed to the windows and pushed them wide, letting the warm summer breezes blow in. Sitting on the cushioned window-seat, she surveyed the view over the well-tended gardens. A year ago she had looked from these same windows, a confident twenty-year-old without a care in the world. Then, literally overnight, everything had changed.

She could remember every detail of that hot summer evening, for it was etched indelibly on her memory—it had been the last time she had seen Morgan...

*   *   *

It all began with Una, as so many things tended to. Her mother had long ago given up all pretence of fidelity. She lived most of the time in London, but periodically she would descend into the wilds of Hampshire. Usually when she wanted something. This particular occasion she had presented Ralph with a *fait accompli* house party for the weekend. The guests had been noisy and self-indulgent, and Leigh would have avoided them herself if Ralph hadn't retreated to his study. She had felt there ought to be at least one responsible member of the family keeping an eye on things, and with Morgan still away she had had to stay.

Unfortunately, though, that had brought her into contact with Gerald Villiers, an ex-army type whose wife was the only female present whom Leigh felt any sympathy for, because she had a genuinely warm nature and clearly suspected she had only been married for her money. Leigh had no doubts herself because Gerald pursued her relentlessly all weekend, whenever his wife was out of sight, seeming only to take encouragement from her constant rejections. The crunch had come on Sunday night. By then she had had more than enough. She had taken the first opportunity to escape, slipping into the darkened library where she hoped to find sanctuary. But before she had even taken one relieved breath, he'd materialised behind her and she hadn't been quick enough to evade his arms.

'So this is where you got to, darling,' he'd crooned in her ear. 'Clever of you not to turn the light on.'

'Wasn't it?' Leigh retorted drily, wishing she had an arm free to box his ears.

'We don't want to be interrupted now, do we?' he went on, hands greedily wandering everywhere.

Leigh gasped in outrage. 'Especially not by your wife!' Her scorn was cut off by another gasp.

Gerald chuckled. 'Grace has gone to bed with a headache.'

'Does she know what you get up to?' Leigh demanded, fighting a losing battle to get free that left her breathless.

'Hardly.' He sounded smugly pleased with himself. 'She'd stop my allowance if she did! But let's not talk about Grace,' he urged.

Leigh realised then that she would never get anywhere by force, because he was far too strong. She would have to use guile. If it was the last thing she did, she'd put an end to Gerald Villiers' philandering! She stopped fighting, and with an unseen grimace said seductively, 'All right, what shall we talk about? Us?'

He groaned. 'Oh, baby, now you're talking my kind of language. I knew your playing hard to get was just a game. God, you're so beautiful! Have you any idea how much I want you?'

With his hold relaxed, she was able to bring her hands to rest on his chest. 'O-oh, I think so,' she drawled, brain working furiously. 'But I don't come cheap, Gerald. If you want me to be —generous—you have to be generous too.'

'Just name your price, darling. Anything you want, it's yours.'

Creep! Well, not for much longer. She put a hastily devised plan into action. Her voice became cajoling. 'You know, I've been admiring Grace's diamond bracelet all weekend.'

That stilled him. 'What?'

'You did say anything,' she reminded him, pouting, then added an edge to her voice. 'Are you an Indian giver, Gerald? I don't think I like that,' she said coldly.

'No, no! If you want it, it's yours.' Just as she expected, he reacted quickly to her apparent cooling off.

Leigh could almost have laughed if she hadn't felt sick with disgust. 'I'll be *very* grateful, darling—afterwards,' she promised.

His eagerness was revolting. 'Stay right there. Grace will be asleep by now. You shall have the diamonds, darling, and then we'll have a party of our own.' He pressed a wet kiss to her lips and let himself from the room.

Leigh wiped the back of her hand across her mouth with distaste. And then we'll see what your wife has to say, you louse! she thought grimly. When he came back with the bracelet, the only party he'd be attending was a lynch one, for she had every intention of going straight to Grace and showing her just what her husband had done.

Her thoughts had gone no further when, with an abruptness that blinded even as it startled her, a light was switched on. She turned, blinking as, from a high-backed wing-chair, a figure rose. Alarm quickly turned to a surprised delight.

'Morgan! I didn't know you were there!' she exclaimed, starting to smile. He hadn't been expected this weekend and his arrival was a pleasant surprise.

He didn't smile back. In fact he looked at her with ice in his eyes. 'No, by God, but I'm glad I was. It was an education long overdue to hear that delightful little scene,' he told her scathingly.

If he had struck her, she couldn't have been more stunned. Never had he spoken to her with such—chilling contempt. For an instant it blinded her to the fact that he had completely misunderstood what he had heard. Eyes wide, face still pale, she said, 'Oh, that. I can explain. Gerald——'

'Spare me the sordid details,' Morgan interrupted harshly. 'Believe me, I heard enough to know exactly what's been going on. You had me fooled completely, and that hasn't happened often. I've been away too long, it seems. You've changed.'

A hollow pit seemed to have taken the place of her stomach. She couldn't believe they were having this conversation. 'If you mean I've grown up, then of course I have. I couldn't stay a child forever!' She attempted to jolly him into a laugh, but failed, and felt an icy chill run up her spine.

Morgan's face became set with grim lines of distaste. 'It would have been better if you had. I liked the child you were, Leigh. I thought there was a chance for you, but I was wrong. Not only do you look exactly like Una, you've shown your true colours at last. I suppose it was naïve of me to expect differently. You'll barter yourself for the things you want. How many Geralds have there been already? God knows how you manage to still look so innocent, but that's probably how you keep my father hoodwinked as to what's really going on.'

'Morgan!' she protested faintly. Attacked from a quarter she least expected, she didn't know how to protect herself. 'Stop it!'

His lip curled. 'I wish I could, but it's too late. You'll forgive me if I don't stay to watch the next touching scene, but I don't have the stomach for it.' He was past her and heading for the door before she could will her legs to move.

'Wait.' She caught him at the door. 'You've got it all wrong.'

His eyes dropped to where her hand clutched his arm and she snatched it away, colour burning her cheeks.

'Have I? Wasn't it you I heard demanding a diamond bracelet in return for your favours?'

Leigh swallowed back a groan. 'Yes, but——'

Again he wouldn't let her finish. 'But nothing. You've admitted it. There's nothing more to say. You'd be wasting your time, just as I've clearly wasted mine all these years. I thought better of you, but you weren't worth the effort.' With that biting condemnation he reached for the door-handle. 'Now, if you'll excuse me, I have to get to the airport. I'm flying out to the Gulf. You'll be pleased to know I won't be around to put a damper on your—entertainment!'

Leigh stirred, glancing back into the room with a frown. It had been like having your favourite pet turn on you and bite you. She had never told anyone about that scene, because it had hurt so much that Morgan could so easily think badly of her. The evidence had been damning, but even so, she had thought he'd known her better than that.

She did now what she had done then: walked to the nearest mirror and stared at her reflection. One accusation standing out above all others. The likeness had always been there, but maturity had defined her features. The classic bones with their covering of alabaster skin, the black hair, slightly slanting green eyes and that shockingly sensual mouth were all her mother's. They could have been sisters.

Yet that was where any similarity began and ended. Inside they were totally different. There wasn't an amoral or mercenary bone in the whole of Leigh's body. She had always believed that Morgan knew that, just as Ralph did. But that brief meeting had shaken her to her roots.

Her first reaction had been a deep hurt, close to a sense of betrayal. Morgan should have known she was only acting. Gradually, though, common sense had made her realise that anger of the type he had shown had no room for past knowledge. It had been a spur-of-the-moment reaction, and she had to make allowances. When he had had time to cool down and think, he would know just how foolish he had been to doubt her for a second.

Only it hadn't been easy to accept that he had gone away with such a very low opinion of her. It had never happened before and it had preyed on her mind for months. She had wanted him home so that she could make him understand. Instead there had only been a long silence broken by one or two letters addressed to Ralph, in which she had barely been mentioned.

No wonder, then, that the news of his imminent arrival had done little to cheer her. Allied to that was a tangle of emotions she couldn't unravel. But at the top, she did know she wanted to have his approval again, and it was this, more than anything, that made her so edgy now. In the past, as a child, when she had annoyed him, she had always managed to make him smile again. But she was no longer a child. Would a smile be enough? By sheer accident she had let him down and she felt that deeply, because she had always striven to let both men know how much she appreciated their trust.

All of which had her on a see-saw, and it wasn't comfortable. She stared hard at her reflection before giving it a piece of her mind.

'You're a fool, Leigh Armstrong. He knows you. Of course he does. He was shocked and angry, but that's past. Just you wait and see. He'll be the same Morgan he always was, and all this agonising will have been for nothing! You see if I'm not right!'

She looked away quickly before the doubts could set in, going to the bed and stripping off the bedspread. There was plenty of work to keep her occupied. With any luck, she wouldn't have to think about Morgan at all.

A faint hope, as it turned out, because Morgan was the favourite topic of conversation over the next few days. So when the actual day of his arrival dawned, bright and sunny, Leigh was glad that Toby Franklin telephoned, and she invited him to go riding. It would be the perfect way to rid herself of some of the tension that was coiling inside her.

The Franklins were old friends who lived the other side of the village. Toby and Morgan were of an age, so Leigh had known him a long time. They were good friends, nothing more, who enjoyed each other's company. Toby had gone into law, like his father, and had built quite a reputation for himself. But, as Leigh was fond of telling him, she didn't hold that against him.

Toby didn't own a horse, but he was a good rider and usually rode Morgan's gelding at least once a week to keep him exercised. He drove over early and they set off, enjoying a couple of leisurely hours, giving the horses a good gallop before taking a rest on a nearby hilltop where the views were breathtaking.

Leigh sat down with a sigh that drew Toby's attention. He studied her slightly pensive profile for a while, then said, 'All right, what's up?'

She tugged ruthlessly at a piece of grass. 'Morgan's coming home today.'

'Ah!' Toby's expression was knowing. 'That explains why you haven't been your usual chirpy self. I should have guessed. When Morgan's around you only have thoughts for him.' His voice dropped mournfully, causing Leigh's head to spin round, her face apologetic.

'Oh, Toby, I'm sorry. I didn't mean to be rude.'

He laughed, eyes dancing. 'You weren't, and I was just teasing. We all know how you feel about Morgan. I always found it rather touching to see you following him about like a faithful hound, taking whatever he said to heart.'

Leigh pulled a face. 'That was a lousy trick! And I wish everyone would stop reminding me about how I used to behave. I've grown up now.'

Toby's grin grew wider. 'I can see that! And most beautifully, too!'

Leigh bit her lip and glanced down at her hands. 'How can I be beautiful when I look like Mother?'

All at once Toby sat up straighter, his face serious. 'Hey, kid, what's wrong?'

She raised a diffident shoulder. 'It's nothing really, just . . . lately I've wondered if people will hold the way I look against me.'

He took hold of her shoulders and gave her a little shake. 'That's the craziest thing I've heard you say. The answer is no. All anyone has to do is look in your eyes to see you have a warm heart and a good soul.'

Leigh gave a half-embarrassed laugh. 'I didn't know you were so poetic. I do believe you're a romantic at heart.'

His face sobered. 'Ah, you've found out my secret. I wish everyone could be as observant,' he added wryly.

Leigh's eyes widened. 'That sounds like woman trouble to me. Do you want to talk about it?' she offered with ready sympathy.

Toby shook his head. 'Not yet, but thanks for the thought. You're a good kid, Leigh.'

She squared up to him. 'Not so much of the kid.'

Laughing again, he climbed to his feet and pulled her up after him. 'Woman, then. I'd like to know what old Morgan makes of you now!'

Leigh rolled her eyes. 'Don't ask! We had a few words on the subject before he left last time.'

'Words!' His ejaculation was loaded with surprise. 'You two had a fight? I don't believe it! I'm sure I'd have noticed if the sky had fallen in!'

'Very funny! And it wasn't a fight, just words.'

Toby came to give her a leg up. 'Words, fight,' he said, laying a friendly hand on her thigh as he looked up at her, 'whatever, Morgan will forgive you. Everyone knows he'd forgive you anything.'

Leigh watched Toby mount and hoped 'everyone' was right. Anyway, the long ride home cleared away the remaining cobwebs and they were both laughing when they dismounted at the stables and handed the horses over to the stable-lad.

'You'd better say hello to Ralph before you leave, Toby,' Leigh advised as he slipped a friendly arm along her shoulders. 'Or you could stay to lunch.'

'Can't, I'm afraid. Dad's expecting an important client and he wants me there. I'll be cutting it fine as it is. You can tell Morgan I'll probably call in next week to see him, though.'

They were on the short cut through the shrubbery when voices suddenly reached them on the breeze. Leigh's heart invented a new dance, and the butterflies in her stomach started dancing it too.

'You can tell him yourself,' she said breathlessly.

A few steps further on the path twisted and brought them to the edge of the sweeping lawn. On her own, Leigh might have paused, but it was impossible with Toby beside her. She was glad, though, of his closeness as they stepped out into the sunlight and drew the attention of the two men sitting in deck-chairs. Her eyes went straight to Morgan, and her spirits rose when she saw him looking so relaxed and unguarded.

Her step was light as she walked towards them with Toby beside her. They had stopped talking, waiting for them to reach where they sat. She was very much aware of Morgan's regard, but then, she was watching him with equal intensity. It wasn't until they had come a great deal closer that she could actually see the look on his face. He might be smiling, but there was an altogether different expression in his eyes. Leigh saw that same contempt there as she had that night, and there was anger too. Her own smile faltered instantly, and only remained as a weak imitation because Ralph was present.

It was Toby who actually spoke first, taking his arm from about her shoulder to offer his hand to his friend. 'Great to have you back, Morgan.'

'How are you, Toby?' Morgan shook hands, his smile broadening.

'Oh, mustn't grumble.'

'Are you staying to lunch?' Ralph repeated Leigh's invitation.

'Sorry, I'm going to have to love you and leave you. Dad's got a client coming. I'm late now, so I'd better shoot off. Drop in next week, Morgan, Mum and Dad will love to see you.' Turning to Leigh, Toby ruffled her hair. 'Thanks for the ride, sweetheart. Right then, I'm off. See you later.' With a cheery wave of his hand he strode off across the lawn and disappeared around the side of the house.

Leigh wished he hadn't gone, especially when her eyes encountered Morgan's narrowed blue ones. She was at a loss to know what she had done to have him look at her so. All she had done was cross the lawn. Unless the past year had made no difference. But it was hard to believe that his anger had remained that long. This was something else—but what?

Crossing to her stepfather's chair, she bent down to kiss his cheek. 'I'm sorry I'm late, Ralph.' Her voice sounded husky, unused, and she cleared her throat nervously. This was ridiculous!

He smiled up at her as she straightened. 'You're not late, my dear, it was Morgan who got here early. Aren't you going to go and say hello to him?'

Her eyes flickered and met icy blue ones for a charged second before dropping away. It hurt her almost physically to look at him and see his disdain. More so because she didn't know the source. Ralph was so cheerful that he didn't seem to notice the constraint in the air. Not wanting to upset him by refusing, which she had half a mind to do, she crossed to the younger man.

'Hello, Morgan, welcome home,' she greeted as evenly as she could, and bent to kiss him too, because she always had, and Ralph would expect it. He flinched as her lips touched his cheek, and Leigh felt her colour draining away and her throat closed over. She straightened painfully, drawing in an unsteady breath, green eyes clouding in dismay. 'Did you have a good flight?' The banal question was all she could manage because her brain seemed to have ground to a halt. She was forced to glance at him for his answer and found only mockery.

However, he answered politely enough. 'Calm, but boring, like most long flights. It feels good to be back here.'

'You should have come before,' she told him as she settled herself at Ralph's feet and rested her arm on his knees. His hand came to rest on her shoulder, instantly comforting. 'You must have had some holidays.'

Morgan's eyes narrowed. 'At the time it seemed a better plan to get the work finished as quickly as possible. Now I'm inclined to think I should have come, at that,' he said coldly.

Leigh was scarcely able to credit what her brain was telling her. Whatever his reasoning, she figured in it, and not to any advantage either. All she could do was stare at him dumbly.

'Morgan tells me he's back home permanently,' Ralph interrupted the silent interchange of their eyes. 'No more gadding about around the world. He's only taking home projects. It will be good to have him back with us at last.'

Knowing exactly how much he always missed his son when he was away, Leigh gave him a fond smile. 'We'll be a family again.' The words choked her. She wanted to cry like a child, but she didn't know why. Only that it felt as if the family was falling apart, not coming together.

Ralph tugged a lock of her hair and tipped his head at his son. 'What do you think of our Leigh, Morgan? Turned into a right little beauty, hasn't she?'

Leigh held her breath as Morgan let his eyes rove over her. Almost instinctively she braced herself—and was proved right the next second.

'She's getting more like her mother every day,' he pronounced at last, and watched her eyes widen in appalled understanding. He smiled. 'And where is my stepmama?'

His father shrugged, long past being hurt by Una's defection. 'In London, I assume. Leigh keeps me company these days.'

'I'm surprised she isn't in London too.'

Leigh didn't need a high IQ to work out his meaning, and slowly inside her hurt was superseded by anger. Green eyes clashed fiercely with ice-blue ones.

Unaware, his father chuckled. 'I keep telling her she shouldn't waste her time with an old fogey like me, but she insists she enjoys it. Can't think why!' His eyes teased her and she laughed, albeit unevenly.

'I wouldn't have thought it was so very difficult to understand,' Morgan drawled, making Leigh sit up straighter.

'What's that?' His father turned to him sharply, as if he had suddenly felt something of the atmosphere that hung over them.

Morgan was equal to it and laughed easily. 'Come off it, Dad. Knowing you, you've been angling for sympathy, and Leigh's too kind to say no.' As an explanation it clearly satisfied Ralph's mind, but not Leigh's, and he knew it. He hadn't meant that at all. She wasn't surprised when seconds later he sat up. 'I think I'd like to stretch my legs a bit. I've been sitting for hours. Coming, Leigh?'

'Yes, you go along and keep him company, Leigh,' Ralph urged before she could open her mouth to refuse. 'I'm going to have a nap before lunch. I'll see you both later.'

When he closed his eyes pointedly, there was nothing for Leigh to do but accept the hand Morgan held out to help her to her feet. They walked down to the bottom of the garden where a gate set into the hedge gave entrance to the woodland. Morgan held it open ostentatiously for her to pass through, and she did so with her nerves giving off warning signals like crazy. She couldn't ever remember feeling so uncomfortable in his presence before, and she rummaged in her mind for something to say to break the increasingly unnerving silence.

'Ralph was very proud when you won that design award, Morgan. He's started a scrapbook. We cut out all the articles in the magazines and pasted them into it. He missed you terribly. Though he'll never say so, it hurts him when you go away. He's not young any more, you know.'

'I'm well aware of my father's age. As for missing me...' he glanced at her sideways, smiling mockingly. 'I have it from his own lips that you more than made up for my absence.'

'Oh, rubbish!' she snapped, his mockery getting to her. 'It's you he wanted. You're his son and he loves you.'

'Believe it or not, I love him too,' Morgan replied curtly as they reached the glade by the stream. He stopped her move to cross the stepping-stones by taking her arm and spinning her round. The coldness of his expression made her shiver in the sunlight. 'All right, just what's going on between you and Toby?'

'Toby?' Leigh blinked at him in complete surprise.

Morgan ground his teeth. 'Yes, Toby. He was all over you like a rash, and you weren't pushing him away, Leigh. Is he the latest mark? Just what are you expecting to get out of sharing your favours with him? A ring to match the bracelet? Or has somebody else already provided that?'

Leigh paled as the questions were barked at her, their allusion patently clear. 'How dare you suggest such a thing? That's the most sickening, disgusting thing I've ever heard!' she cried, revolted.

'Exactly my own opinion when I saw the pair of you. I had no idea just what was going on behind my back, but I should have guessed. Like mother, like daughter. Toby's a wealthy man, and there will be more later, as your avaricious little eyes would know.'

Her gasp was a mixture of anger and disbelief. 'For your information, Toby is in love with someone else!'

Morgan laughed. 'That never stopped your mother— why should you be any different?'

Her hands balled into fists. 'Because I'm not my mother! How could you even think...? Toby's my friend, for God's sake!'

His look was shrivelling. 'You must have learned a lot from Una over the years. Enough to know you can crawl into Toby's bed without fear!'

He would probably have said more, but she slapped his face so hard he reeled slightly before regaining his balance. Leigh stared at him, so hurt at the tone he had used to her that she felt sick. Sickened, too, by his dreadful allegations. For his part, one hand explored his cheek as he stared down at her, smiling malevolently.

'So, the kitten has claws, has she? Like to play rough, do you, Leigh? So does your mother. She tried that on me once, too, but I didn't oblige. I don't think she's ever forgiven me. But you need teaching a lesson, darling. Toby's like my brother. Get your claws out of him, or, I promise you, you'll regret it.'

Leigh's mind reeled with what he was telling her. Her mother had made a play for Morgan? The idea was disgusting, but she didn't doubt it. Knowing her mother, she found it all too horribly possible! As for his unfounded charges about Toby, they made her fume.

'You have a mind like a sewer, Morgan. Whatever you say, I've only ever seen Toby as my friend, and I'm not going to stop seeing him because you've suddenly gone mad! How can you even suggest that I would... would...?' She couldn't bring herself to say it.

'Have you looked at yourself in the mirror lately?' he demanded scornfully, ignoring her declaration.

Her hands balled into impotent fists. 'There's more to me than the way I look!' she cried angrily.

Morgan laughed without humour. 'Believe me, I know it. I've seen it all before and I won't watch it happen again.'

His blindness brought tears to her eyes. 'I am not my mother,' she gritted out between her teeth.

'You forget, I've seen you in action. Or is it so long ago now that you've forgotten Gerald? Do you still have the bracelet?'

'No.' It had gone straight back to his wife as she had planned. It hadn't been a pleasant scene, but she had been glad she'd done it. Her mother had been furious, naturally, but Grace Villiers had thanked her, and that had made it all worthwhile.

'What happened? Did his wife catch him and put a stop to your little game?'

'I'll tell you what happened if you're interested,' Leigh bit out hardily, still wanting, even after this, to clear up the mistake.

'I'm not,' he returned savagely. 'Honeyed words come easy to the likes of you and your mother. You're as like as two peas, and both rotten to the core. There's bad blood in you, I only have to look at you to see it.' He seared her with his contempt.

This time when her hand lashed out he saw it coming and was ready for her. He caught both her wrists with ease and twisted them behind her back, the movement bringing her body hard against his and stealing her breath away.

'Not this time, you don't,' he muttered angrily, controlling her efforts to get away with ease. 'Once is all you get.'

'Let me go!' she ordered fiercely, using her feet now that her arms were clamped tight. She'd fight him to the last ditch. He couldn't say such things to her and get away with it. She hated him for saying them. Lies, all of them!

But all she managed to do was wear herself out, until finally she collapsed against him, panting for breath, eyes clamped over weak, angry tears. Somehow she had to make him listen. There had to be a way through. Swallowing, she raised her head to gaze at him through eyes that looked like rain-washed emeralds. 'Morgan.' At the sound of his name, he glanced down, and their eyes met.

She saw as well as felt him go still. Watched the light blue of his eyes darken as he stared down into her upturned face. A strange mixture of emotions flitted across his face—a blend of shock and surprise—and something else he had an inner battle with. She saw, to her confusion, the exact moment when he lost the fight. Realisation dawned.

Eyes darkening in alarm, she tried to struggle free. 'No, Morgan. No!' It was too late.

His head swooped and his mouth claimed hers. Leigh caught her breath at the shock of it—at the heat and the unexpected tingle of excitement that shivered along her receptive nerves, and kept her there, unresisting when she should have been fighting to be free. She whimpered as her head fell back under the force of his kiss, eyes closing on a mixture of beauty and pain. His mouth was exploring hers, moving restlessly, his tongue tracing the delicate contours, seeking an entrance with an expertise that dazzled the senses.

Trembling from pure shock, Leigh was flooded with a sweet, hot rush of sensation that melted her bones instantly, and her lips parted to his insistent pressure. The gliding invasion of his tongue in ever deepening, silken strokes was an irresistible invitation. An ache started to throb deep down inside her and she felt her nipples surge to life. At the same time she was vitally aware of Morgan, too. His body heat scorched her, they were pressed so close together.

The noises of stream and woodland faded. There seemed to be no other reality but this, and she was helpless to do anything but return the kiss in full measure. Feeling her response, Morgan's arms tensed, then he released her hands, one arm sliding down to gather her closer, the other hand gliding up beneath her hair to frame her head and deny her the right to refuse the deep, sensual demand of his kiss.

Her arms went around him, clinging to the only stable thing in her reeling universe, and for wildly passionate seconds everything was forgotten but the unexpected pleasure they discovered in each other.

Leigh's mind was totally shattered by the revelation of that embrace. When Morgan tore his mouth away from hers, she could only stare up at him dazedly from beneath heavy lids. They were both breathing as if they had just run a gruelling race. But, even as she watched, she saw horror and disgust sweep all signs of passion from his face.

'No!' He thrust her away so hard she almost fell. 'No, by God, not me! I loathe and despise all that you and your mother stand for. I won't be another scalp on your belts. One fool in this family is enough! I'd have to be really desperate to accept what you're offering, Leigh. Save it for some other poor fool.'

With another all-encompassing look of disgust, he turned and walked away from her with long, angry strides.

Unable to utter a word, Leigh watched him go, raising one trembling hand to press against her lips. She could scarcely believe what had just happened. Yet one thing was clear: he blamed her for it. But how could she be responsible for a kiss she hadn't expected in her wildest imaginings?

Turning away, Leigh rested her forehead against the roughened bark of the nearest tree. That kiss had changed everything, for how could she ever forget their response to each other? She was aware of him now as a man. A stranger who was no relation, and who could draw from her a wildly physical response. Yet there was no point in remembering it as anything but a momentary aberration. Not with the accusations Morgan had levelled at her.

How she wished the moment could be undone. She didn't want this. She wanted things the way they had always been. But that was impossible now, wasn't it? She closed her eyes. Lord, she didn't know what she wanted now. Morgan had lifted the lid of a Pandora's box, and for the life of her she didn't know whether to be glad or sorry.

CHAPTER TWO

IT WAS impossible to avoid dinner that first evening, for Ralph had organised it into a celebration. If her gaiety was brittle, Leigh didn't think Ralph noticed. He certainly didn't seem to find anything wrong with Morgan's mood either, but Leigh's sensitive radar knew that he was far from being the relaxed figure he pretended. He barely glanced her way, and when he did it was with a look of intense dislike. She hadn't seen him since he'd left her by the stream, and it was clear that in the interim he had pushed all blame for what had occurred totally on to her shoulders. The unfairness of it rankled. She had been prepared to take some blame, but not all. It was hard to hold back her angry words, but she did because she didn't want to spoil Ralph's happiness. She was never more relieved than when Ralph finally took Morgan away to his study for a quiet chat, leaving her the opportunity to escape to her room.

There she sat and waited for Morgan to come up to bed. When he did, she intended having a private talk with him. That decision had been the result of a long afternoon of thought. Like it or not, she had to try and change his opinion of her, because they couldn't go on as they were. His accusations were unfounded and she would tell him so.

As for the other, it made her go hot and cold just thinking about it. The only way to cope with it was to treat it as a mistake. Something that had happened out of the heat of anger and wouldn't happen again. They had to get themselves back on a level footing and put an end to this madness that seemed to threaten to tear their lives apart.

It was a long time before she heard his footsteps along the passage, followed by the opening and closing of his door. She didn't give herself time for second thoughts but quickly left her own room and went to tap softly on his door. It was a second or two before the door opened and then Morgan was looking down at her coldly. For a second neither spoke, then he smiled.

'It's a little late for visiting, or are you into nocturnal calls?'

It wasn't a promising start, but Leigh hadn't come this far to turn back. 'We have to talk.'

One eyebrow rose. 'Do we have anything to say?'

Her lips pressed together tightly. '*I* have something to say,' she said determinedly.

He stood back. 'Then you'd better come in.'

Said the spider to the fly, she thought as she stepped inside. Morgan shut the door and leant back against it, waiting. Leigh licked her lips. Now she was here, it seemed difficult to start. She sighed and faced him.

'Morgan, what's happening? We never used to fight like this. We always used to be able to talk to each other.'

'Mm. Now I wonder how I'm supposed to react to that?' he mocked back, and Leigh's temper rose.

'Will you stop that? This isn't a game! I'm being serious. I don't want things to be like this.'

Morgan pushed himself away from the door, slipping his hands into his trouser pockets as he prowled towards her. 'What do you want, Leigh, or can I guess?'

He was referring to that kiss, she just knew it, and her teeth snapped together. 'No, I don't think you can! I want things to be the way they were between us.'

He laughed. 'Before I discovered the truth, you mean?'

Biting back a retort, she took the opening he offered despite his scorn. 'Oh, Morgan, there was no truth to discover. You overheard something and jumped to conclusions. I can explain about Gerald Villiers. He——' She got no further because Morgan took one angry step towards her, gripped her shoulders and shook her till her head snapped painfully on her neck.

'Get this straight. I don't want to hear anything about the men in your life. Not another word. You may have been able to twist me around your little finger when you were a child, but those days are gone. Now I only go by what I see, and I don't like it, not one iota.'

Ungentle hands spun her round to face the mirror, holding her there when she tried to break free.

'You see what I mean? You're your mother all over again, and that attempted seduction this morning merely proves my point. Things can never be as they were because I'm not a fool. Now, I suggest you go back to your room and think again, because I'm on to your little games now.'

Leigh stared at his reflection, eyes darkened by pain. 'You're wrong, Morgan. I didn't want any of this. I only want us to be friends once again. Is that so impossible?'

His face hardened. 'Totally. We aren't the same people we were then. You can never go back, didn't you know that? You took a chance and lost; now you must live with it.'

She felt herself very close to tears but refused to let a single one drop. 'I think I hate you. How can you do this? We were a happy family once.'

'You should have remembered that before you got greedy. It's a lesson you had to learn. You can't have everything just because you want it. Now go to bed. We're both tired, and this is getting us nowhere.'

Morgan let her go and turned his back, and there was something implacable about the set of it. Leigh swallowed hard. 'All right, I'll go. You're wrong, but I can't convince you. Before I do, I want your agreement that Ralph shouldn't be hurt by any of this. If it has to be a fight, it's just between us.'

He glanced over his shoulder. 'I couldn't agree more. Dad deserves a bit of peace. You stay out of my way, and I'll stay out of yours.'

Leigh left with that, for there was no reason to stay any longer. She had never believed that her world could deteriorate into this state in so short a time. There was no reasoning with him. He had made up his mind and wasn't even prepared to give her the benefit of the doubt. Well, she wasn't going to show him how much that hurt. A small but defiant seed of rebellion started to germinate inside her.

Over the next couple of days, avoiding Morgan didn't prove too difficult. When they did meet, Leigh did her best to act naturally. Morgan viewed her politeness with mocking amusement, treating her to his own special brand of crocodile courtesy. His lips might smile and his words might be mild, but his eyes accurately recorded his dislike.

She knew as well as he did that they were only staying this side of open warfare for Ralph's sake. It was their very mutuality of purpose which gave Leigh confidence that they were doing a good job of hiding the true nature of affairs between them. So it came as something of a surprise to hear Ralph sigh exasperatedly at breakfast one morning when they had been more than ordinarily polite.

'What's the matter with you two? You used to help me relax at mealtimes. Now all I get is indigestion. Have you had a row?'

Leigh's eyes flew to Morgan's, received no help, then quickly passed on to his father. 'A row? What makes you think that?' She laughed uneasily.

Ralph gave them both an old-fashioned look. 'I may be getting old, but I'm not senile yet. You've never been this polite as long as I've known you. You're trying too hard, both of you. What's got into you now?'

'You're imagining things, Dad.'

'Oh, am I? Then you see nothing wrong in the fact that if one of you walks into a room, the other walks out of it? Or am I imagining that too?' Ralph finished with heavy irony.

Leigh flushed, because it was true. She reached out to touch his hand. 'I'm sorry. You weren't supposed to know.'

'Not know?' her stepfather challenged. 'Don't you
think I'd have just a tiny doubt when two people who
used to spend a great deal of time together don't exchange more than two words? What's more, it only
started when Morgan came home.' He looked squarely
at his son.

Leigh, looking at Morgan too, saw the angry set of
his jaw and hastily stepped in to avoid the coming explosion. 'You can't blame Morgan, not entirely. It was
my fault too. You see we . . . had a difference of opinion,
and neither of us is prepared to back down. We aren't
talking to each other.'

Ralph looked from one to the other in disbelief. 'I've
never heard of anything so childish! I never expected it
of you. And I'll tell you this—adult you may be, but I
won't have my children behaving in this way in my house.
Whatever this silly squabble was about, you'll make it
up now.'

'I can't believe this!' Morgan declared incredulously.
'We're not children!'

His father banged his spoon down on the table-top.
'I'll treat you how you behave, my boy. I'll have you
know I hold you entirely responsible for this.'

Morgan laughed. 'I might have known it. You always
were a sucker for a pair of beautiful green eyes. I thought
you would have learnt by now.'

Ralph's brows rose. 'Learnt? Learnt what?'

Leigh paled and turned accusing eyes Morgan's way,
alarmed at the turn the argument had taken. How could
he have said that? For a second it seemed as if he was
about to ignore her, but then he sighed and raked a hand
through his hair.

'Nothing,' he said irritably. 'Forget it. I don't want
to argue with you, Dad. Besides, I thought you wanted
to end an argument, not start another?'

'You've got me so I don't know what I do want!'
Ralph exclaimed testily, then caught sight of Leigh's
anxious expression and his face softened. 'Except seeing

you two friends again.' The glare he reserved for his son. 'Well?'

Morgan pulled a wry face and turned to Leigh, one eyebrow lifting mockingly. 'What do you say, Leigh?' he asked softly.

She met that look with a raised chin. 'I'd like us to be friends.'

A confession which had his smile broadening. 'How can I fight you both? Friends it is,' he declared smoothly. 'You'd better give me a kiss or Dad will never believe we mean it.'

He might have sounded teasing to Ralph, but Leigh knew better. He hadn't stopped fighting at all. The thought of a kiss, even a perfunctory one, shivered along her nerves. She doubted she could carry it off with the necessary aplomb. 'Oh, I don't think friends need to do that,' she said, smiling grittily. Morgan said nothing, he simply gave his father a helpless shrug, which put her in the wrong. Realising she would be forced into it anyway, she quickly rose to her feet. 'But seeing as it's you,' she added, smiling sweetly. She walked round behind his chair and dropped a kiss on the top of his head. 'There! Now are you satisfied? You'd better be, because I have plans.' She made herself sound chirpy, though her heart was thudding. 'If you don't need me this morning, Ralph, I think I'll exercise Bones.' Usually they worked in the morning when it was cooler.

'You go ahead, my dear. I plan to go over those research notes you typed for me.'

Relieved, Leigh made her way to the door, stopping only briefly to drop a kiss on Ralph's cheek. 'I'll see you later, then. Don't work too hard. I'll get Rose to bring you some coffee.' With a brief glance at Morgan's inimicable face, she left.

She ran up to change into ankle boots and an old pair of jeans, but because it was already very warm she exchanged her sweater for a white vest-type T-shirt. Then she took the back stairs out of the house and used the short cut down to the stables. The grey mare was pleased to see her, whickering as Leigh rubbed her sleek nose in greeting. As she saddled her up, she crooned away to the friendly animal, and didn't hear the footsteps approaching. The voice behind her came as a complete surprise.

'This is Bones?' Morgan drawled, and she swung round with a start to find him lounging against the stall wall, hands tucked into the pockets of his jeans. Though she didn't want to, she couldn't help noticing that he looked far, far too attractive for her peace of mind. 'I thought her name was Silver Dream.'

Lowering mental shutters on this unwelcome awareness, Leigh put the horse between them and concentrated on running her hand down the sleek nose. 'It is, but she's a bit of an old lazybones these days, so I've come to call her Bones.'

He looked vaguely amused. 'Like most females, she'll accept anything if the price is right. In her case, I assume it's sugar.' Pushing himself away from the wall, he crossed to run his hand down the mare's neck. 'What do you do for my father, Leigh?'

Her head came up and she met his blue gaze. 'I'm Ralph's research assistant. He's writing a book, a history of the Fairfax family. I check sources and type up his notes for him.'

'A book? This is the first I've heard of it.'

'Are you surprised?' It was her turn to mock. 'You've hardly shown much interest in your father this last year! Perhaps he got the idea you didn't want to know.'

He didn't like that, but the truth of it was inescapable. 'Damn!' he swore, raking an angry hand through his hair. 'It wasn't like that.'

She had drawn blood but found she had no taste for it. Her soft heart forced her to take the sting from the words. 'No, it wasn't. He knew that. Anyway, you're home permanently now, that's all that really matters.'

Morgan looked sceptical. 'You can't expect me to believe that it matters to you too, Leigh.'

'I don't see why not. I want to see Ralph happy,' she declared honestly, and made towards the tack-room door. But Morgan's large figure was there before her, leaving only a small space to scrape through. She was forced to stop and look up at him.

'Doesn't my coming home make you happy too?'

Leigh dragged in a ragged breath. He was goading her, and enjoying it, the devil! 'Yes!' she retorted acidly, and pushed past him into the tack-room. What a joke! How could she ever be really happy again? She reached for her hat with jerky movements, and turned—to discover just what a tactical error it had been to come in here, because Morgan was now blocking the whole door, and there was nowhere for her to go.

'Liar. You've probably been dreading it, knowing I intend to curb your avaricious tendencies.'

Oh, God, she felt so battered and bruised by his constant barbs! Her sigh was defeated. 'And if I told you you're wrong, you wouldn't believe me, would you?'

'Exactly.'

Damn, he was so smug!

'You realise, of course, that we can never be friends as Dad wants,' he said now, blue eyes raking her from head to toe.

Leigh's fingers clenched on to the rim of the hard hat. 'I'm not a fool,' she said huskily.

Morgan's lips curved. 'I agreed only because I don't want to see my father hurt any more, and this way I get to keep an eye on what you're up to.' His gaze came to rest on the agitated rise and fall of her breasts. To her utter shame, she felt them respond. It took all her control not to cover herself with her arms and call down more of his mockery. Embarrassment made her reply sharp.

'Is that why you've decided to live with Ralph and not take a home of your own?'

That brought his narrowed gaze back to her face. 'Braydon *is* my home. Nobody is going to run me out of it. It will be mine one day, so, whatever plans you and your mother may have, you can forget them, right now!'

'If my mother has any plans, I certainly have no idea what they are, and I don't want to know. They're nothing to do with me,' she responded tautly.

'Too busy on your own plans? I've a pretty good idea what they are too. It turns my stomach to see you with your claws into Toby,' Morgan declared scathingly.

That was one slur too many. She couldn't keep taking the hurt without fighting back. Unfortunately it pushed her into rashness. 'What's the matter, Morgan? Jealous?'

Leigh regretted the words the minute they left her lips, but by then it was far too late. She knew she was wise to be fearful when she saw the savage glitter in his eyes. He was absolutely furious at that charge. Her heart quailed because she knew he was about to exact some fitting revenge.

Morgan prowled towards her and instinctively she backed away until brought up short by the wall. Halting mere inches away, he put one arm out to rest on the wall, blocking any avenue of escape; the other hand he raised to cup her cheek, letting the ball of his thumb rub back and forth over her lips. He smiled slowly. 'Now why should I be jealous when I can have all that for the asking—if I wanted it?'

With a surgeon's precision he cut her, and Leigh gasped at the pain. 'That's not true!' she denied hoarsely, hating his arrogance.

'Isn't it?' he taunted silkily. 'Let's see, shall we?'

Do something, her brain urged as she watched his head lower, don't let him do this. Sluggishly her hand came up to ward him off. 'No, you mustn't.' It seemed hard to breathe, as if the room were airless.

'Admit it, Leigh, you've wanted me to do this.'

Miserably she shook her head, yet she remained mesmerised like a rabbit, unable to save herself from the inevitable. The truth was exactly as he had said—she wanted him to kiss her, had wanted it ever since the last time. Shaming though it was, she just couldn't seem to help herself.

Without prompting, her lids lowered, lips parting as she waited for the touch of his. It never came, only a low, mocking laugh that smote her to the heart.

'Yes . . . any time I wanted.' The words were a breath over her lips before he very pointedly moved away from her. 'But I don't want it, not at any price. So thanks, darling, but no, thanks.'

Leigh didn't see him go, he was just a blur, but she knew when he was gone and dashed the bitter tears from her eyes angrily. She had asked for that, but it didn't stop the ache in her chest.

Jamming the hard hat on her head, she collected Bones, mounting nimbly out in the yard and setting off along the path through the woods at a brisk pace. It was good to have the air rushing past her hot cheeks, and it dried the last of her tears. The mare was willing, but she was getting on in years now, and Leigh drew her thoughts away from her own misery to stop on the brow of a hill and give them both a rest.

It was a favourite look-out point, but today she wasn't interested in the view. Her thoughts swerved inevitably back to Morgan. What was he trying to do to her? Life was going to be unbearable, because she couldn't see the situation getting any better.

Her vision blurred again, and she wiped furiously at her eyes. Oh hell, where was her pride? Why didn't she just say to hell with him and go? Because she was damned if she'd let him get her on the run. She wasn't at fault. She had done nothing she need feel guilty of. So far he had won all the points because she had let what he said hurt her. Emotionally she was still in the past, where Morgan was an adored older brother. Well, she'd have to let that go for good. Those days were gone forever. He was her enemy now, not her friend, and if he wanted a war he could have one. She wasn't going to lie down any more and let him walk all over her! She didn't care

now how badly he thought of her, because she didn't
want his approval. In her opinion it wasn't worth having!

The decisions bolstered her flagging confidence in the
nick of time, and Leigh grimly remounted and rode
slowly back home. She spent a long time grooming the
mare, finding comfort in the rhythmic movements that
blanked her mind of all thoughts. Finally she made her
way up to the house and took a leisurely shower before
changing into a cotton sun-dress. Subconsciously she
knew they were all ploys to avoid Morgan. Her decision
was one thing, but her armour wasn't all it should be
yet. However, when she went down to lunch, she found
she need not have gone to such trouble. Morgan had
gone out, and wasn't expected back until later.

She spent the afternoon in the study, typing up Ralph's
manuscript. She had no worries that Ralph would ask
her why she was so silent. When he was caught up in
his research, he was lost to the world. They worked in
harmony until, at four, he glanced up at the clock and
called it a day.

'I'm going to take Martha Fairfax's diary out on to
the terrace for tea. I think I've found something interesting here about George the Third. Are you coming?'
he asked her, picking up the slim volume one of his
female ancestors had written so meticulously two cen-
turies ago.

Looking up from the page of notes she was studying,
Leigh smiled and shook her head. 'I think I'll just finish
this off. Another hour should do it.'

'Very well, my dear. I'll get Rose to bring you a cup.'

She smiled her thanks and delved once more into the
notes. Ralph's discoveries made fascinating reading, and
she was so absorbed in them that she lost all track of
the passage of time, and only vaguely registered the telephone ringing out in the hall.

'Aren't you going to answer that?'

Her head flew up at the sound of Morgan's voice, and
she found him standing at the open french door,
watching her. 'Damn it, must you always creep up on

me? How long have you been standing there?' she demanded, more angry at the traitorous way her heart had
leapt at the sight of him than the shock he had handed
her.

'Long enough. If you aren't going to answer it, I'd
better do it,' Morgan returned, and, walking into the
room, picked up the extension on his father's desk. He
listened for a second or two then turned to her, eyebrows
lifted mockingly.

'Patrick Healey for you, Leigh. Another admirer?' he
drawled. 'Just how many do you have?'

'How high can you count?' The retort shot from her
lips tartly. Inwardly, however, she groaned. Patrick
Healey was a friend, but even she had to admit he had
a reputation with the ladies that positively stank. At one
time he had persistently asked her out, not believing that
her no meant no. Finally, though, he had accepted defeat
and they had fallen into an easy friendship instead. They
went out occasionally, but there were no strings to the
relationship. They enjoyed each other's company, and
that was all. In fact, Leigh had discovered a side to
Patrick that she doubted very few people knew existed.

Ralph certainly saw only the bad side of him, and she
expected Morgan to be the same. Which made it the
worst time for Patrick to choose to ring her. She encountered Morgan's look of open amusement and her
temper, extremely volatile since his return, rose accord-
ingly as she went across and snatched the receiver from
him. She knew what he was thinking. If he expected a
femme fatale act, he'd get one, and no apologies. She
only hoped Patrick would understand.

'Hello, Patrick,' she breathed welcomingly, and produced a smile for Morgan's benefit. 'How are you?'

There was a moment of stunned silence at the other
end of the line, then a startled voice said, 'Is that you,
Leigh?'

He sounded completely thrown and she couldn't help
the husky laugh that escaped her. 'Oh, I'm just fine.
Never better,' she continued airily.

'There can be only two reasons for this strange conversation—too much sun or somebody is there with you,' Patrick observed drily.

Acutely aware of Morgan watching and listening, and irritated that he didn't go away and give her some privacy, Leigh continued flirting outrageously. 'Oh, yes, you're so right. I'd love to have dinner with you.'

At the other end, Patrick laughed. 'What I'd give to be a fly on the wall there! If I take you to dinner, will you tell me what's going on?'

Leigh was mightily relieved that Patrick had caught on so quickly. She saw Morgan's brows rise interrogatively and smiled brilliantly before turning her back on him. 'Of course, you know I love to dance too. What time?'

'Leigh Armstrong, this had better be worth dinner,' Patrick advised with a laugh. 'I'll pick you up at seven-thirty,' he added, and rang off.

Leigh replaced the receiver slowly, taking time to compose her features that tended to break into a grin as she imagined Patrick's astonishment.

'Does my father know the sort of man you're running around with?' Morgan enquired from behind her. 'If memory serves me correctly, Healey has the morals of an alley cat.'

She faced him then, a satisfied smile hovering on her lips and a challenging glint in her eyes. She crossed her arms defiantly, head tipped. 'According to you, so do I, so you can't seriously be concerned about my reputation.'

'Oh, I'm not,' Morgan returned smoothly, and Leigh was glad her hands were out of sight so he couldn't see them curl into fists at that. 'I'm just surprised my father lets you go, seeing you, as he does, as his little ewe-lamb.'

'Ralph knows better than to interfere in my life.' Because he knew he could trust her. An instinct his son didn't possess. 'I'm nearly twenty-one, old enough to make my own decisions and look after myself.'

'Yes,' Morgan mused cynically. 'An instinct no doubt learnt in the womb. You Armstrong women always land on your feet. Perhaps it's Healey who deserves my sympathy.'

Leigh fought the instinct to claw at him like the spitting cat he likened her to. Unfortunately, he was close enough to her to see the message in her eyes. His own flashed back a warning equally strong, and, though she hastily attempted to back away, it was too late.

Morgan caught her to him, laughing grimly all the while, pinning her arms to her sides with his own arms about her, holding her there until she should wear herself out struggling to escape. It was a hot day and he had unfastened several buttons of his silk shirt, and suddenly her lips brushed against the warm, moist male flesh at the base of his throat.

They both froze. Beneath her lips a pulse suddenly started to throb wildly. It was so tantalisingly close that she couldn't stop the tip of her tongue from seeking it out, and her senses leapt as she heard Morgan's sharp intake of breath.

Slowly she tipped her head back so that she could look at him. He was pale, but the blaze in his eyes was hot and fierce. He wanted her. He wanted her with a passion as explosive as her own. He hated her for it, but it didn't stop the wanting.

Hadn't she read that knowledge was power? Now she discovered her power was immense. All she had to do was touch him. She tried it, pressing herself closer, feeling his response in the hardening of his body, the deepening of colour in his eyes. She drew in a shaky breath, and raised her head the fraction needed to press her lips against his. She had never taken charge in a kiss before, and it was heady. She began rubbing her lips on his burning ones, tracing their beautiful line with her tongue until he gasped again and she slipped inside, to taste and tantalise him the way he had her. When her tongue met his, he flinched, then met her challenge as if unable to do anything else. It was a duel that shivered along her receptive senses, and from which she was the first to withdraw.

She stared up into a face flushed with the dull heat of desire. 'Not at any price, Morgan?' she taunted him with his own words. 'You want me.'

'Yes, I want you,' he agreed in a husky voice that sent a shiver through her. 'But there's no pleasure in the knowledge, only an overwhelming self-disgust. Yet I'd take you, lose myself in you without a qualm if you ever tempted me like that again. Remember that, Leigh. You may think you've caught me in your web, but you haven't. I'd stay there only until I'd achieved my own satisfaction, then nothing you could do would keep me. I'm too strong for you. So don't ignore this warning unless you're willing to accept the consequences.'

'And they are?' she asked scornfully.

His eyes narrowed. 'That I'd use you until I was sated of you once and for all.'

Leigh laughed even as a lead weight settled in her stomach. 'And what makes you think I'd let you?'

Morgan's smile was taunting. 'You couldn't stop me. You wouldn't want to. You're a slave to your own sensuality. You let the stormy sea of your passion drive you from shore to shore, leaving your human flotsam behind you. But not me. I'm indestructible. It's you who'd break. So be warned and find yourself another victim.'

She was as white now as he had been, her victory now tasting bitter. 'You don't believe that I could want only one man?' she charged in a thin voice.

He laughed. 'With your pedigree? Not a chance.'

'You could be wrong.'

'And the moon could be made of green cheese!'

As usual he had defeated her, but she refused to let him see. So she produced a smile he'd expect from the woman he thought she was. 'How wonderful it must be to be right all the time,' she mocked as best she could. 'You can let me go now, Morgan, I'll be good.'

That had Morgan laughing in sardonic amusement. He had just released her but hadn't moved away when the door was suddenly thrown open.

'Leigh, I've had an idea about Martha's...diary.' Ralph's voice tailed off as he saw the pair of them standing so close as to be touching. 'What's going on here?'

Morgan stepped back and grinned at his father. 'Leigh had something in her eye. I was just getting it out for her,' he explained, tongue in cheek. 'Can you see better now?' he asked her meaningfully.

She set her jaw, her smile every bit as insincere as his. 'Perfectly, thank you.'

His eyes mocked her. 'Good, then I'm off to change for dinner. Enjoy yourself tonight.'

Ralph followed his son's departure, frowning heavily. 'What did he mean?'

With Morgan gone, she felt as deflated as a pricked balloon, and rubbed her forehead tiredly. Fighting with him could never be called a cinch! Yet she felt better for at least scoring some points. 'Oh, just that I'm going out to dinner tonight, that's all,' she said flatly.

'Anyone I know?'

What she hadn't felt like telling Morgan was that she was fully aware Ralph wouldn't like to hear she was going to see Patrick Healey and, not being up to another argument right now, she was deliberately evasive. 'No, just a friend.' She glanced at the clock. 'I really ought to go and get ready too.'

'Leigh.' Ralph's voice stopped her at the door. 'Did you really have something in your eye? Not that I don't believe you, but...' He smiled ruefully at her puzzled face. 'If you must know, I've always nurtured the secret hope that you and Morgan would make a match of it.'

She felt floored. She had never guessed, and it had certainly never occurred to her. Marry Morgan? 'Oh, Ralph...that's...'

He held up a hand. 'I know, an old man's folly. Still, I thought I'd let you know you'd have my blessing if...'

He shrugged and sighed. 'But I'm keeping you from your date. Off you go, my dear.'

All at once she felt as if she could cry, and didn't know why. 'I do love you, Ralph. You've meant the world to me. I'll always be grateful that you took me in and gave me a place in your heart. But I've never thought of Morgan in that way. I'm sorry.'

There was a suspicion of moisture in her stepfather's eyes, and he coughed. 'So am I, my dear, but don't let it trouble you. Off you go now, or you'll be late, and be sure and enjoy yourself.'

Poor Ralph, she thought, as she mounted the stairs. Did Morgan guess at his father's impossible dream? Somehow she doubted it. If he had, he would have laid that at her door too! What a complicated mess life was. Marry Morgan? Hah!

Leigh was on the front steps waiting for Patrick when he drove up to collect her, and she slipped into the car before he could get out.

Patrick was tall, blond and tanned, with the plastic good looks of a male model. He ran his eyes over her appraisingly as she joined him, a habit she hadn't been able to break him of. She gave him an old-fashioned look as she smoothed down the skirt of her sky-blue dress.

'Mmm, you look good enough to eat,' he declared appreciatively.

She laughed. 'The deal was dinner, and I'm not on the menu.'

Patrick moved away with a chuckle and started the car. 'One dinner coming up. After that, it's your turn.'

He had booked a table at a fashionably expensive restaurant not far away. They chatted over dinner, and it wasn't until the coffee arrived that Patrick sat back and demanded an explanation.

With a sigh, Leigh idly stirred her coffee. 'If you must know, it was Morgan. He made me so angry. He's got some bee in his bonnet that I'm a *femme fatale*. When you rang——' She broke off with a shrug.

'You wanted to put his nose out of joint,' Patrick supplied for her.

Leigh pulled a wry face. 'Something like that. Are you mad?'

'Intrigued. You're normally a very contained person.'

'I know, but he's got the knack of rubbing me up the wrong way.' Leigh groaned, then afforded him an apologetic smile. 'Still, I shouldn't have used you.'

Patrick grinned boyishly. 'Forget it. What are friends for? Besides, it gave me a good excuse to take you out. So why don't you finish your coffee, then we'll go and trip the light fantastic, as per instructions? Prince Charming has come to the rescue. Cinderella shall go to the ball, and the devil take Morgan Fairfax!' he declared extravagantly, and Leigh shook her head, laughing.

It was well past midnight when he finally drove her home. He steered the car quietly up to the house, stopping in the shadows and switching off the engine. Much to Leigh's surprise, he turned to her, sliding one hand along the seat behind her, the other coming to rest on her knee.

'Patrick! Behave yourself! Just because——' she began to remonstrate, only to be interrupted.

'We're being watched,' he told her in a conspiratorial whisper.

'What?' Anger was a bubble inside her as she glanced over his shoulder and saw the front door of the house was open, a tall figure silhouetted in the light. Morgan! Incredulously, she realised he was waiting up for her—as if she were a fifteen-year-old! How dared he!

'Of all the nerve!' she spat furiously.

'Want to give him something to think about?' Patrick murmured, drawing her attention back to him.

She saw the gleam of amusement in his eyes and grinned grimly. 'It would be a shame to disappoint him, wouldn't it? Let's make it a clinch to end all clinches!' she declared, and threw herself into the seemingly torrid embrace with enthusiasm. She felt nothing—not that his kiss was unpleasant, but there was no spark to fire her blood. It was proof, had she needed it, that they could never be more than friends.

When Patrick lifted his head moments later, he was laughing under his breath. 'That must have got to him. Has he gone?'

Leigh looked towards the now empty doorway. 'Yes,' she confirmed, freeing herself with a faint sigh. 'Thanks for dinner, Patrick, and for your help.'

'Any time. I'll give you a ring, OK? You can tell me all the sordid details.'

Climbing out, Leigh laughed. 'Thanks again. Good-night, Patrick, drive carefully.' With a wave she walked to the house, mounted the steps and went in.

Morgan hadn't gone far, only a yard or two inside. She stared at him for a moment, hating his cool mockery.

'Did you enjoy yourself?' he asked blandly.

She raised one eyebrow. 'Did you?'

His lips curved. 'Not nearly as much as you appear to have done. Your lipstick's smudged.'

She lifted her hand to her lips and smoothed their outline with her finger. 'Never mind, I'll have to remove it anyway.'

'He'll never marry you, you know. The way he's going, he'll have run through his money by the time he's thirty.'

'Then it's just as well I don't intend to marry him,' she observed sweetly. 'I have my eye on bigger fish.'

Morgan's expression darkened. 'Toby?'

Leigh smiled. 'That would be telling. Oh, and by the way, it was sweet of you to open the door, but I'm not a child who has to be waited up for.'

Morgan strode past her to close and bolt the door. 'My father didn't think so when he found out who you were with,' he replied tartly.

Leigh turned, aghast. 'You told him?'

Straightening from shooting the bottom bolt, Morgan rested his hands on his hips. 'I had no idea it was such a secret.'

'I'll bet you didn't!'

He shrugged, but there was a glitter in his eye. 'You'd lose. However, he seemed bound and determined to wait up for you himself. Apparently he thought you might be in need of protection. I only persuaded him to go to bed by saying I'd wait up instead. For someone who *says* she cares about him, you cause my father far too many worries.'

'He wouldn't have been worried if you hadn't told him,' she pointed out shortly.

'Anyway, from what I saw, it was a false alarm. You had everything under control,' he drawled scathingly.

Her smile was icy. 'In which case you can safely go to bed now.'

'After you,' he returned with mock gallantry.

Jaw set, she strode angrily to the foot of the stairs. 'What do you imagine I'm going to do, sneak out the back way?' she threw over her shoulder.

'It's been done before.' His harsh reply came from right behind her, and she knew he was referring to her mother again.

Her fingers whitened tensely about the banister rail as she bit back a smarting reply. He wouldn't listen anyway. Feeling deathly tired, she made her feet begin the long climb. 'Good*night*, Morgan,' she said pointedly, without looking back.

'Goodnight, Leigh.' His voice floated mockingly up to her. 'Pleasant dreams.'

Pleasant dreams? She must have had some, but for the life of her she couldn't remember what they were like any more.

CHAPTER THREE

To LEIGH'S relief, Morgan spent the greater part of the following week in London. He had decided to work from home now that he was based in England, and one of the outbuildings was being converted into a studio. Meanwhile he was busy making contacts and having meetings with potential clients. With his work now well known, he had taken on junior partners, and they would still be working out of the London office. All of which meant they saw very little of him as he left early Monday morning saying he would be home some time on Friday.

Patrick rang her in the middle of the week to invite her to a party on the following Wednesday. Nothing had been said at breakfast the morning after her date with him, except for Ralph's one brief comment that he hoped she knew what she was doing. She knew it was pointless trying to alter his opinion of Patrick. She loved Ralph, but when his mind was set there was no budging him. In that, he and his son were alike.

Unfortunately, Patrick's call had come at the wrong time. 'I'd have loved to, but I won't be able to make it. It's my birthday, you see, and Ralph will have arranged a special surprise.'

Patrick lowered his voice to a husky drawl. 'I could arrange something special for your birthday too, darling,' he murmured suggestively.

'Self-praise is no recommendation,' she countered crushingly, and he groaned.

'Cruel woman! But I forgive you. Ring me if you change your mind, beautiful.'

She laughed. 'I'll do that. Bye.' She put the receiver down knowing there would be little chance of that hap-

pening. Birthdays were always special events in the
Fairfax household.

At dinner on Thursday Ralph surprised her with the
news he would be going away for a few days, perhaps
even a week. He had business in London, then he intended to hunt down a few leads he had come across in
the diaries. He left early on Friday morning. Leigh
cleared up a backlog of notes, and then, unexpectedly
finding herself with free time, rang Toby and invited him
to lunch.

They ate out on the terrace as it was a beautifully warm
summer's day, and Leigh had been chatting away for
some time before she realised Toby was only half-
heartedly listening. When she stopped mid-sentence he
didn't notice, and with a sigh she reached her hand out
to him, saying, 'Why don't you tell me about it, Toby?
If it was trouble at work, you'd leave it there, so it has
to be a woman. *The* woman?'

He took her hand with a self-conscious laugh. 'You're
right, of course. It's so ridiculous. Ask me a point of
law and I'll give you an answer, but I just don't know
what to do about Helen.'

'Helen? That's her name? What does she do? Do I
know her?'

'You ought to. She runs the stables over in Stapleford,'
he confessed.

Leigh couldn't hide her surprise. 'Good heavens!
Helen Peterson? Now I think about it, she'd be wonderful for you, Toby. You've so much in common. I've
always liked her. It was sad when her husband died,
leaving her with the two little boys, but she's managed
really well.'

'I know, I've handled some legal work for her. That's
how we met. I think I fell in love with her the first time
I saw her,' he admitted softly.

'Then why the sad face?' Leigh prompted.

'She doesn't seem to notice I'm alive. I keep finding
excuses to pop over there, and she always seems pleased
to see me, but—that's all.'

'Have you tried asking her out?'

He pulled a face. 'I keep meaning to, but...'

'You chicken out. You have got it bad, haven't you?' she laughed kindly. 'Where's the Toby who was never afraid of anything?'

'Damn it, Leigh, a man likes to get some encouragement!'

'You really are an idiot. Hasn't it occurred to you that a young woman with two young children might not feel as if she's attractive enough for any man? Who wants to be landed with a ready-made family?'

Toby looked angry. 'That's rubbish! I would. They're great kids.'

'Then why don't you tell Helen that, and ask her to dinner. I'll babysit for her,' Leigh declared strongly. 'Faint heart never won fair lady, you know. Go for it. I'll bet she's just waiting for you to ask.'

Toby took a deep breath. 'All right, I will.' He let his breath out again in a sigh. 'You'd better be right.'

Leigh giggled. 'It's really funny seeing you so unsure of yourself. A big strong man like you!' she teased.

He grinned back. 'Wait until it happens to you, my girl!'

They both laughed at that, and Toby sprang up to round the table and drop a light kiss on her lips.

'Am I interrupting something?' A bland voice broke in on their amusement, and they both turned to see Morgan standing in the doorway.

Of all the moments for him to walk in, this had to be the worst, Leigh thought, as colour rose in her cheeks. She met his set expression knowing she must look as guilty as hell, but there was nothing she could do about it. Except, that was, carry the moment off with aplomb.

'Hello, Morgan. You're home early. Have you had lunch?'

He must have discarded his jacket and tie in the house. With his shirt unfastened at the neck and the sleeves rolled up, he looked devastatingly attractive, and Leigh couldn't stop her heart from missing a beat. Now he came forward, hooking out a chair and sitting down.

'Rose is bringing me a sandwich with your coffee,' he answered shortly, looking from Leigh to Toby, who now sat on the coping. 'You seemed to be enjoying yourselves when I came in.'

Unaware of the tensions between the other two, Toby grinned. 'She's a great kisser, your sister,' he declared cheerfully, winking at Leigh who stared at him aghast.

Her 'Toby!' was swamped by Morgan's ground out, 'Is she indeed?' He turned steely blue eyes on her. 'Due to practice, no doubt? Perhaps I ought to warn you, Toby, that they're something my stepsister's pretty free with. Don't take them seriously, will you?'

Toby looked understandably surprised. 'Are you warning me off?' he asked incredulously.

Morgan shrugged casually. 'Just offering you a piece of advice.'

Now Toby frowned. 'It's not like you to come the heavy brother, Morgan.'

'*Step*brother,' Morgan corrected pointedly.

Leigh's cheeks paled at that blunt disavowal of any family relationship. It made her angry, too. 'Toby was only joking,' she said repressively, glancing at him for support.

He responded immediately, but hardly the way she expected. 'No, I wasn't. I'll have you know, Morgan, I think a very great deal of your sister—*step*sister.'

Leigh stifled a groan of despair. She knew what Toby was doing even if Morgan, from the look on his face, didn't. He was doing it to get a rise from his friend, but it was only making the situation worse.

'Stop it, Toby, it isn't funny,' she warned.

'I agree,' Morgan interjected. 'If you think I'll let Leigh marry you, Toby, you can think again.'

Toby stood up. 'If I wanted to marry her, I would. You wouldn't be able to stop me,' he said belligerently.

'Try it and see,' Morgan suggested bitingly.

Leigh's fist hit the table, rocking the crockery. 'Stop it this instant!' she ordered, boiling inside at the way they were behaving. 'If you'll stop bickering like a pair of children, *I've* something to say. After all, it's me you're arguing about.'

Toby had the grace to look shame-faced, but Morgan merely turned a freezing blue gaze on her. Though she saw it, she was too furious to be intimidated.

'Go ahead, I'm listening.'

She gave an angry laugh. 'You always listen, you just don't hear. If you weren't so—so damn conceited, you'd realise Toby was baiting you. You're barking up the wrong tree. We're friends, that's all. And as for you,' she turned her attention to the other man, 'I know you think you're championing me, but there's no need. You see, Morgan isn't protecting me from you. It's the other way around!' The look she threw her stepbrother was fulminating.

Morgan remained silent; it was Toby who showed his surprise.

'Protect me? What on earth does he think you're going to do to me?'

'Eat you for breakfast,' Leigh retorted acidly.

'Why, for heaven's sake?'

'Because she's her mother's daughter,' Morgan spoke up at last.

'Leigh, like Una?' Toby laughed, then sobered rapidly when he realised Morgan was serious. 'I ought to punch you on the nose just for saying it!' he said coldly. 'Leigh's as honest as the day is long, and you damned well know it!'

'Naturally I'd expect *you* to say that,' Morgan grated tersely.

Toby's cheerful features had become quite forbidding. 'You've changed, Morgan, and frankly, I don't like it much. If I find you've been upsetting Leigh with these ridiculous notions, I'll come back and finish what we nearly started. In the meantime, try growing up.' His tone was scathing, but he was smiling when he turned to Leigh. 'Sorry, sweetheart, me and my big mouth. I must go. I'm late already. See me out?'

Relieved to get away from the nail-biting tension, Leigh walked with him to the door. 'I'm sorry you had to go through that, Toby.'

'No sweat. Are you OK, though?' he asked in concern.

Leigh smiled. 'I'm fine. Morgan will calm down soon.'

Toby looked grim. 'He'd better. I don't know what's got into him. Remember, if the idiot gets too much, you can always come to us.'

'I'll remember, but I doubt I'll need to.'

'You know best. Anyway, thanks for lunch—and the advice.'

'Just act on it. I'll keep my fingers crossed. Now go before I get an angry phone call from Uncle Henry.'

Toby left with a wave. Leigh closed the front door with a sigh and reluctantly made her way slowly back to the terrace. Morgan was standing at the parapet drinking coffee. At the sound of her footsteps, he turned.

'I hope you're proud of yourself,' she declared shortly. 'You very nearly came to blows with the best friend you've got. I hope you're going to apologise.'

A nerve ticked away in his jaw. 'Why? Because he looks at you and just can't see straight?'

She stared him out. 'I suppose it couldn't be you who needs glasses?' she queried sarcastically.

'I've got twenty-twenty vision. That's good enough to see through any smokescreen you try to put up. Toby might be fooled, but he doesn't know you the way I do. After what I saw today I don't think I came home a moment too soon.'

Leigh had to laugh at his sheer arrogance. 'You're incredible, you really are. I've done nothing. What is it going to take to get you to believe me?'

'For a start you could leave Toby alone. No invitations to secluded little lunches—and no kisses.'

So, they were back to that again. 'Sometimes you can be a real pain in the neck, Morgan Fairfax. I think Toby's right, you do need to grow up,' she stormed, and hurried from the terrace before she was tempted to give in to tears.

That confrontation left them barely talking to each other. Morgan spent the weekend shut up in his studio, which suited Leigh perfectly. With the express purpose of keeping well out of his way, she went up to London to do some shopping on Saturday, but although she spent the day there she came back with very little. On Sunday she played tennis with friends at the local country club, but her game was off, and she returned home in the late afternoon feeling out of sorts with herself and the world.

She dined alone, as she had the night before. Morgan had disappeared without a word, but she heard him arrive home in the small hours as she lay tossing sleeplessly in her bed. She spent the next hour wondering where he could have been, and consequently woke in the morning feeling completely unrefreshed.

After a solitary breakfast, she took herself off to the pool to sunbathe, stretching out on a lounger in a skimpy emerald bikini. It wasn't long before the somnolent heat of the day had her teetering on the edge of sleep.

It was a loud splash that brought her lids up again, and she looked towards the dazzling blue water of the pool to see two strong arms cutting the surface in a powerful crawl. She didn't need to see the dark head to know it was Morgan—her senses had already relayed that information to her brain. She lost count of the number of lengths he did before finally pulling himself from the water in one lithe movement. Leigh's mouth went dry as he stood there in the sunlight like some Greek god, water running from the planes of his chest and abdomen, across minuscule briefs that left nothing to the imagination, and down over the powerful thighs of his long, straight legs.

She couldn't count the number of times they had swum in the pool together. Enough so that seeing him barely clothed was no novelty, but now she was seeing him through new eyes. Her stomach lurched and knotted on a powerful surge of primitive awareness and she couldn't drag her eyes away. He was the most beautiful thing she had ever seen, she thought helplessly. Then his head turned, the dark hair plastered to his skull, and he looked at her, and she knew from the glitter in his eyes that he had been fully aware of her appraisal. That he had blatantly posed for her, as if to say, is this what you want?

If she had had any power in her legs she would have got up and run, but she felt as weak as a kitten as Morgan prowled around the pool towards her like some proud jungle cat. For a moment he loomed over her, scanning her flushed face, then hunkered down beside her, bringing his body excruciatingly close.

One finger came out to trace the heat in her cheeks, then trailed on down her neck, taking her breath from her as he drew a line to where her breasts rose and fell on agonised breaths.

Lazy blue eyes lifted to hers. 'Hot?' he queried huskily.

She swallowed down a groan and slapped his hand away. 'Yes.'

He smiled slowly. 'Did you enjoy the show?'

'Wasn't I supposed to?' she returned waspishly.

Morgan's smile merely broadened as he ran his eye over the shapely length of her. 'You'll burn in this heat if you're not careful. You should put cream on,' he observed, meeting her eyes again.

'I already have,' she told him shortly, nodding to where the bottle lay beside her.

Morgan picked it up. 'Turn over and I'll do your back for you.'

The mere idea turned her bones to water. 'That won't be necessary, thank you,' she refused sharply.

His brows lifted. 'Scared?' he jeered softly.

Oh, God, how could she admit that she was when he had done this very thing for her time out of mind? But never when she was feeling so very femininely aware of him as a man. Yet to refuse would be too revealing. So, with disjointed movements, she turned, mutely presenting her back to him, burying her head in her arms. He must have heard her sharp intake of breath as he released the catch on her bandeau, and she could almost feel his mocking grin. She prayed for the sophistication he credited her with to carry off the next few torturing minutes.

It *was* torture, the glide of his hands upon her velvety skin. A sensual torture by a master of the art. His fingers traced her spine down to her tiny briefs, then trailed up her ribs, fingertips skimming the sides of her breasts as he went. To her shame she could feel her breasts swell, her nipples becoming taut and aching—dear God, aching for him to slide his hands beneath her and ease their tumescent need.

The thought was so shocking her nails dug into her palms as the nerves in her belly churned wildly. How could this be happening to her? her dazed mind asked. She who had always remained so cool and controlled. To lose that now at Morgan's hands was frightening. On and on he went, until she was ready to scream. He had to stop now, or else ... or else ...

'That's enough, Morgan,' she ordered, her voice cracking on the command.

He stopped, hands splayed out across her hips. 'You don't really mean that,' he contradicted, voice husky and mocking.

Holding on to the bandeau, she turned over. 'I do. I ...' Her voice tailed off as she met the mesmerising blue of his eyes. So deep she could drown in them.

Morgan reached out a hand to tug the bandeau from her numb fingers and dropped it to the tiles. 'I know what you want, what you need,' he whispered throatily.

She couldn't move, couldn't think—could barely breathe as he scooped her into his arms and stood up. 'Morgan?'

He half smiled. 'Going to fight me, Leigh?' he asked, and the smile deepened as she dumbly shook her head. 'Good.'

He carried her easily—right off the side of the pool. Her eyes registered the shock of falling through space, but it was nothing to the shock-waves that the cold water

sent through her overheated system. She surfaced,
gasping for breath, stormy emerald eyes seeking him out.

Morgan was at the other end of the pool, eyes dancing
with amusement. With a lithe twist, he heaved himself
from the water. 'Enjoy your swim, darling. It should
cool you off.'

Damn, damn, damn! What a stupid, stupid fool not
to have seen that coming.

'Mor-gan!' Rose's voice carried to them from the other
side of the shrubs that shielded the pool area.

He turned, wiping water from his eyes. 'What is it,
Rose?'

'Telephone for you,' the housekeeper explained
without coming closer.

'I'll be right with you,' he called back. Grabbing his
towel from the chair where he had left it, he cast Leigh
another mocking glance. 'Need any help getting out?'

'Oh, buzz off, Morgan!' she snapped and turned her
back on him, gritting her teeth as he laughed and went
away with a further recommendation to her to keep cool.

Cool! If she could only get her hands on him, she'd
give him cool! she thought direly. Then, realising what
she was thinking, she laughed harshly. To do that she'd
have to touch him, and the results so far were that every
time she did she went up in flames. He knew it, too, and
that gave him a hold over her that she couldn't recip-
rocate. Because he could control it and she couldn't. It
was so—degrading—to suddenly find herself wildly attracted to someone who thought so ill of her.

With a groan she pushed herself away from the side
and began to swim length after length until her body
was exhausted, and the ache he had aroused merely an
ember deep inside her. At last she clung to the side,
breathing heavily.

She prayed for Ralph to come home soon, before she
did something really stupid. What that could be, she
didn't know, only that it seemed to be hovering just over
the horizon. The catalyst was obvious though.

'Oh, damn you, Morgan, why did you have to come home?'

Her birthday dawned bright and fair, but Leigh awoke with none of her usual expectancy. Since Monday she had been feeling edgy and listless by turns, and this morning the latter won. She couldn't even explain why she experienced these uncomfortable fluctuations. She only knew she couldn't drum up enthusiasm for anything. The world was painted a uniform dun colour. The only bright spots seemed to be her clashes with Morgan, and to find herself looking forward to them was to verge on insanity.

They were thoughts that made her sleep uneasy and her appetite virtually non-existent.

Showering, she chivvied herself into being more cheerful, and slipped on her favourite rainbow-hued sundress in the hope it would help. It certainly added colour to her cheeks and highlighted her eyes, she thought, as she brushed her hair until it shone. Yet it seemed a pointless exercise when the only one who would see it was Morgan, and he would probably only liken her to her mother again.

The thought took away any remaining enjoyment, and she went down to breakfast with a heavy weight about her heart. The sight of only one place set at the table made her falter in the doorway before slowly going forward to take her seat. It was ridiculous to feel hurt that nobody was there to celebrate her birthday with her, but she was. There couldn't have been a better way for Morgan to show her how little he cared for her.

But in this she was wrong. He had added a refinement, she discovered, as she opened the cards stacked beside her plate. There was a card from her mother with her usual cheque, a cheeky one from Toby, and one from Ralph promising a surprise when he returned—but from Morgan there was nothing. Leigh double-checked to make certain, then sat there staring at the pile with a lump the size of a golf ball in her throat. There had to be an answer. Surely even he wouldn't be that petty?

Rose bustled in from the kitchen just then, grinning from ear to ear, carrying a gaily wrapped parcel and a card. 'Happy birthday, Leigh,' she greeted warmly.

Leigh accepted the gift with a fleeting smile. 'Thank you, Rose. I hope it's nothing fattening,' she teased, striving to act normally.

'Go on with you, you couldn't get fat if you tried! Now, what do you want for your breakfast?'

'Oh, just toast and coffee, please. Um, has Morgan had his breakfast?' It occurred to her that he might not have left a card if he hadn't come down yet.

'I wouldn't know, lovey. He went up to town late last night and hasn't come back yet,' Rose supplied the information as she bustled out.

That came as a surprise to Leigh, but she had been out herself so it was no wonder she didn't know. She opened her card and present in a distracted mood. Well, his absence gave her another option. When Rose returned with her breakfast, she thanked her for the delicate glass figure that was her gift, then added, 'I don't suppose Morgan left anything for me, did he?' Her glance was unwittingly hopeful.

'Not with me, dear. Didn't he send a card? That's odd. Oh, well, perhaps he's going to bring something back with him,' she suggested brightly, and left again.

Leigh doubted that. The same way she doubted he had genuinely forgotten. Morgan never forgot—unless he wanted to. The knowledge was like a dagger in her heart, tearing a painful wound that ached in a way she had never experienced before. The slight had been deliberate, and she felt it to her soul. She would never dream of inflicting hurt so pointedly. How could he have done it?

Pain gave way to anger. She knew the answer. Because she was like her mother and therefore impervious to everything.

With the thought of food making her nauseous, Leigh left the table, taking her cards with her. She thought of taking them to her room but disliked the idea of Morgan realising why she had done it. So she placed them on the mantelpiece in the sitting-room as always. Jaw set tight, she studied them. Just let him make one comment, and she'd spit in his eye! Just one! As for herself, she had no intention of showing that she'd even noticed she was a card short.

To prove it she went out and didn't return until late afternoon. Only to discover that Morgan hadn't come home yet either. Which made her own absence totally pointless.

So she was just in the right frame of mind, when Patrick rang her to wish her a happy birthday, to say, 'Is that party still on?'

'Changed your mind? That's great. I'll pick you up at eight.'

His enthusiasm brought a determined smile to her lips. Come hell or high water, she was going to enjoy herself. She threw herself into the party spirit. Apparently Patrick had told everyone it was her birthday, and they broke into a chorus of 'Happy birthday!' the instant she walked in. Then they all helped her to celebrate. There was music and dancing, plenty of food and a veritable ocean of drink of all sorts. Leigh drank very little. It wasn't alcohol that put her in a reckless mood, but a growing restlessness inside her. She knew the cause of that too.

It was all Morgan's fault. Why did he have this effect on her? Why couldn't she just not care? Her mother wouldn't, but she wasn't her and never could be.

Patrick drove her home in the small hours. Locking up behind her, she felt too restless to go to bed. Something was missing and she knew what it was—Morgan. All her life, Morgan had been there, watching over her, affectionate and caring, and she missed that. Damn it, what did she have to do to make him love her again? Heavens! Where did that word come from? She didn't mean love, she meant like, of course. She didn't need his love! She wasn't that stupid! Fall for Morgan? She'd need her head examining if she did that. No, liking she'd accept, but what would it take? Plastic surgery and a blonde dye? Hah! Not even that would work.

Depressed, she walked slowly into the sitting-room and poured herself a glass of white wine. Sinking on to the couch, she kicked off her shoes, set the glass on the floor and stretched out.

The sudden invasion of light made her screw up her eyes for an instant, then she sat up slowly, resting her arms along the back of the couch and her chin on her hands. She blinked at the sight of Morgan framed in the doorway, his hair tousled, body clad in a dark maroon silk robe that stopped mid-thigh—and nothing else.

Her pulse went haywire and her mouth was full of cotton wool. Damn him for being so attractive to her! Suddenly she hated him for that, for making her so vulnerable. How she wished she could hurt him the way he was hurting her! It wasn't fair that all the turmoil was on her side. But that was far from true. Morgan wanted her though he hated himself for it. All at once she had the germ of an idea. Why not make him do the very thing he didn't want to do? The thought precipitated the deed.

'Were you waiting for me?' she drawled slowly, deliberately seductive, and saw the sudden sharp focusing of attention in his eyes.

Morgan's hands went into his pockets. 'Do you realise it's after two in the morning? Where have you been?' he asked stonily.

Hidden by the couch, her treacherous body stirred as his movement parted his robe dangerously. 'Are you coming the heavy *brother*, Morgan?' she mocked back, warming to the part.

She heard the soft intake of his breath as he tensed, eyes narrowing warily. 'You're drunk,' he charged disgustedly.

Leigh laughed low in her throat. 'I've been celebrating, certainly, but I'm not drunk. I can still walk the white line. Shall I walk the white line for you, Morgan?' she provoked, softly mocking.

She didn't wait for his reply, but rose gracefully to her feet. There wasn't a line, but the carpet had a distinct pattern, and she followed that, one foot placed before the other, arms spread for balance, small white teeth nipping at her bottom lip as she concentrated.

She came to a halt before him, eyes flashing triumphantly as she looked up. 'There, you see!' she declared, and, with delicate precision, overbalanced. 'Oops!' she laughed as his chest broke her fall.

Then, to her consternation, instead of feeling his arms going round her, saving her, she was sliding floorwards, unable to stop herself from landing in an undignified heap at his feet. When she looked up, it was to find it was his turn to mock.

'Comfortable?'

She blinked, wondering just how the tables had turned so neatly. Then her eyes widened as he came down on his knees beside her, blue eyes glittering, mouth bearing a grim smile. 'What are you doing?' To her dismay, the question wavered nervily.

Firm hands pushed her down on to the carpet despite her resistance. 'I warned you, but you chose not to listen,' he told her, stretching himself out over her so that the weight of his body held her captive. 'So now you have to take the consequences.' His eyes lanced into hers. 'This *is* what you wanted, isn't it?' he jeered.

Her throat closed over. Her eyes sought to find some spark of emotion in his face, but there was none, only a cold determination. 'No!' Her denial was strangulated. How could it have gone so terribly wrong? 'Don't, please!'

Morgan laughed. 'Too late, darling,' he said chillingly, and brought his mouth down on hers.

Leigh went into shock at the deliberate calculation of his lips and hands. There was no passion, no wild desire, only a devastating technique designed to arouse her body leaving heart and mind untouched. And it worked. She didn't want to respond but had no control over her own senses. Morgan knew exactly what he was doing. When he lifted his head to look at her, his eyes were full of a cold satisfaction at seeing her helpless in the toils of her senses while he remained remote.

She tried to turn her head away, but he wouldn't let her, his fingers on her chin clamping her head still.

'Do you still want to carry on the game?' he asked derisively.

She had to swallow a painful lump in her throat to say, 'No.' Misery tightened its fingers about her heart as Morgan rolled off her at once and stood up. She had just been given an object lesson in sex without emotion, and she would never forget it.

'Get up.' Morgan's voice was harsh in command.

Avoiding his eyes she scrambled to her feet, trying to stop the shaking that threatened to make her collapse on the spot.

'The next time Healey leaves you feeling frustrated, don't come to me for satisfaction,' he grated cuttingly.

Leigh's nerves jolted violently. He thought she had tried to seduce him because of Patrick! The idea was ludicrous, and yet far better than that he should guess the real reason. It was her only chance of salvaging some of her tattered pride.

'Don't worry, I won't,' she croaked and made herself face him with a defiantly raised chin. 'Can I go now?'

Morgan smiled grimly. 'I don't want you for anything more,' he responded crushingly.

Painful heat scorched her cheeks. 'I suppose I should thank you for stopping.'

He shrugged indifferently. 'I had no real desire to go on.'

The *double entendre* cut like a blunt knife. That had been all too painfully obvious. Without another word she turned away, heading for the stairs on legs that threatened to collapse under her.

'Goodnight, Leigh… Happy birthday.' Morgan's cool, mocking tones followed after her, but apart from one falter she didn't stop.

Only at the foot of the stairs did she risk a glance back. Through the open door she saw Morgan cross to the drinks trolley and pour himself a stiff measure. He stood and stared broodingly down into the liquid for a long time before finally draining it at one go.

Not wanting to be caught spying, she carried on up to her room then, only to lie sleepless in her bed until sheer exhaustion took her just as the sun began to rise.

Consequently, it was well into the morning when she awoke, with a faintly throbbing headache that reminded her—as if she really needed it—of all that had passed in the dark watches of the night. For the first time ever, she felt as if there was no reason to get up. Morgan now despised her more than ever. What was it that kept making her do one stupid thing after another? Now he'd be even more convinced of her 'true' nature.

Irritably she threw back the covers and padded into the bathroom. A shower did much to revitalise her fighting spirit, and an aspirin set to work on her fuzzy head. Dressed in a black and white print dress, she descended the stairs once more, and made her way to the kitchen where Rose was busy shelling peas.

The housekeeper looked up with a beaming smile and a distinct sparkle of mischief in her eye. 'Well, there is still life in you! Feel like eating?'

Leigh pulled a rueful face. 'Just toast and coffee, please.'

'You're soon served,' Rose declared drily, getting up. 'Go on into the dining-room, I'll only be a minute.'

Leigh pulled out a chair. 'In here will do.'

'It will not. You'll eat in the other room like a lady,' Rose chided with mock severity, and, when Leigh blinked in surprise, shooed her out. 'Go on.'

She went, not a little confused by the scene. The times she had eaten in the kitchen were innumerable. But she shrugged; perhaps it was one of those days. There was only one place set at the table, and beside it sat a small, elegantly wrapped parcel.

For no accountable reason her heart started to thud away and she sat down heavily. Reaching for the package, she twisted it between her fingers, strangely reluctant to open it. She was still staring at it when Rose bustled in with her breakfast.

'Now, young lady, I expect you to eat that. I'm not wasting my time making breakfast so you can leave it on the table!' she chided, crossing her arms. 'Well, aren't you going to open it?' she chivvied, nodding at the gift.

Leigh's fingers were all thumbs as she fumbled with the wrapping, uncovering a jeweller's box which, when she lifted the lid, revealed a delicate gold chain from which hung one perfect tear-drop diamond. She stared at its beauty speechlessly. There was no card, but it had to be from Morgan. He had bought it yesterday, and all the time she had thought... An explosion of sheer joy brought a smile to her lips. In an instant she was pushing back her chair, forgetting her cooling breakfast, as she hurried in search of Morgan, leaving Rose rolling her eyes in exasperation.

He was at his desk when she burst into his studio without knocking, and looked up at once, his frown of surprise turning to a closed expression as he saw her standing there, box in hand. He sat back slowly and waited.

Now she was here, she didn't know what to say. 'Morgan, I... It's such a surprise! But a beautiful one,' she added hastily. 'Thank you.'

He didn't smile and his voice was cool. 'Do you like it?'

His remoteness was undaunting, and she nodded. 'Very much.'

A thin smile crossed his lips. 'I thought you would. I always try to give presents that will be appreciated. Of course, it's not a bracelet, but then, I'm not your lover.'

She went cold, the blood seeming to freeze in her veins at that slap in the face. 'I see. I thought——' She stopped abruptly, looking away and swallowing hard.

'Yes?' his voice prompted softly. 'What did you think, Leigh? That you'd won me over? That I was prepared to forget?'

She glanced up at that, hating the glitter in his eyes. 'No!'

'Good, because that will never happen. With certain people, it pays you never to drop your guard.'

Leigh drew herself up proudly. 'You've condemned me without a hearing. You seem to have passed sentence, too. I think I have a right to know how long I'm to pay for this awful crime I've committed,' she declared levelly.

Morgan's jaw tensed. 'As far as I'm concerned, it's life.'

She had expected no less, but still it cut deeply. She crossed to the desk and set the box on it. 'You'd better take this back, then. It means nothing to me and even less to you. I'd never wear something that was given to me in hate. It would be a constant reminder that the giver was as cold and as hard as the diamond.' She turned then and went to the door, pausing a moment to look back at Morgan's still, silent figure. 'And while you're into not forgetting, remember I tried to explain a number of times, but you didn't want to know. Now *I* don't. Don't ever ask me because I'll never tell you. I've battered my head against a brick wall long enough to finally see sense. You're just not worth it.'

She went out quickly then because tears would have swamped anything she might have tried to say. She meant what she had said—he wasn't worth all this agony. She didn't care any more what he thought. She hated him. Hated him with every fibre of her being.

CHAPTER FOUR

LEIGH caught Patrick's speculative eye and produced a smile for his benefit. Her mood had made him curious but she wasn't about to confide in him. For the hundredth time she wished she hadn't let Toby persuade her to come to this pool party.

She hadn't been in the mood at all when he'd telephoned as she was forcing down cold toast and coffee after that confrontation with Morgan. However, she had been unable to refuse his pleadings when he'd told her that Helen and the children would be there too. It was the perfect opportunity to follow her advice, he had added, and left her with no option but to agree.

Held at the country club, the swimming party was to be followed by a barbecue. All age-groups were present, and the poolside was crowded. Leigh had seen the flaw in Toby's arrangement as soon as they arrived. His cause wasn't going to be helped if he was seen arriving with another woman.

Which was why she was now lying on the sun lounger next to Patrick. She had only had one moment of unease on joining him. She had seen a certain gleam in his eye when he saw her in her bikini, but it had gone in a flash, replaced by his usual friendly grin, and she had relaxed again. They had enjoyed their usual camaraderie all afternoon, and Leigh had done her best to be cheerful, though she knew she hadn't always succeeded.

Across the pool, she was pleased to see that Toby and Helen seemed to be getting on like a house on fire. At least they were happy.

A sudden burst of laughter behind her had her turning in idle curiosity, only to freeze in shock when she saw Morgan had arrived. He was wearing shorts and a tall, leggy brunette. Not that he seemed to mind that she was all over him like a rash—quite the opposite.

'Who's that with Morgan?' Patrick had turned, too.

'I don't know,' she replied shortly, wondering the same thing. Why didn't he tell her to stand on her own two feet?

'Brother, has she got the hots for him,' Patrick declared with a throaty laugh.

'He ought to shove her in the pool to cool off!' she said acidly. 'It's a disgusting way to behave in public!'

'Morgan doesn't seem to mind,' Patrick observed, and Leigh turned away, heart thudding uncomfortably.

She was fighting down the urge to do what she had suggested, and realised shockingly that she was jealous. Green-eyed with it! The knowledge was appalling. She couldn't be jealous, because that would mean...

'Enjoying yourself, Leigh?' Morgan's voice made her jump. As she looked up, her cheeks went a fiery red, then lost colour completely. She had to moisten her mouth before she could answer.

'Yes. Er...I didn't know you were coming.'

Blue eyes gleamed down at her. 'Neither did I. Carole persuaded me.'

Leigh watched his hand caress the other woman's hip and felt her stomach lurch sickly. 'How nice,' she replied thinly.

'I see Toby's found himself a friend. They seem to make a perfect couple, don't they?'

She didn't miss the message but refused to rise. 'I was just thinking that myself.'

'We must have them over to dinner one evening,' he went on, just to make sure she understood.

Leigh looked up. 'You're flogging a dead horse, Morgan.'

One brow rose. 'Am I? I certainly hope so. Well, there's plenty more fish in the sea. Better luck next time.' With a smile to her and a nod to Patrick, he steered Carole away.

Leigh watched them go, a bitter taste in her mouth. To her dismay they joined a group well within her line of vision. It was impossible not to see them every time she looked up, and she wouldn't put it past Morgan to have arranged that deliberately.

She spent one of the most miserable afternoons of her life, hardly knowing whether to be glad or sorry that Morgan spirited his clinging vine away well before the barbecue was due to start. Her mind imagined all sorts of scenarios for their evening's entertainment, which turned everything she ate to cardboard.

When the dancing started she was in no mood for Patrick's urgings to join him. He took exception to her rejection and stalked off to the bar, where he proceeded to drink steadily. Despite his reputation, this was the first time she had seen him drink heavily, and she didn't like it. If there had been anyone else to take her home, she would have left him to it, but Toby had long since departed, so she had no choice.

There were times during that midnight journey when she never expected to reach home at all. That they did finally arrive at the house, she put down more to luck than good judgement, and promised herself that she would have more than a few words with him when he was more sober.

Aware of the distinct chill in the air, Patrick was contrite. 'Hell, I'm sorry. I didn't realise I'd had so much to drink.'

'Didn't you?' Leigh didn't bother to hide her scorn, and felt him turn and look at her.

'Everyone drinks at parties, even you know that.' There was a faint but unmistakable edge to his voice.

She didn't like the way he said it, making her out to be some sort of prude, which she wasn't, but she forbore to tell him that responsible people didn't drink if they were driving. She doubted it would reach the mark tonight.

'I get the silent treatment now, do I?' he said peevishly, then sighed. 'OK, I was wrong, but nothing happened. So give me a break, beautiful, please. Besides, I can't go home like this, the folks would hit the roof. Is there any chance of a cup of coffee?' he ended hopefully.

Why, Leigh thought acidly, hadn't he thought of that an hour ago? She ought to refuse, but her conscience wouldn't let her. If he was to have an accident, she would never forgive herself.

'You'd better come in, then,' she invited reluctantly, climbing from the car.

Patrick followed her into the silent house, where only a low lamp glowed in the hall.

'Where is everybody?' he asked.

'They're all in bed,' Leigh answered, and experienced a stabbing emotion at the idea that it was probably true for Morgan—but whose bed? 'So don't make too much noise. Why don't you wait in here?' She switched on the lamps in the sitting-room. 'I'll go and get the coffee.'

'I'll be as quiet as a mouse.' Patrick grinned at her, and made himself comfortable on the couch.

Leigh headed for the kitchen. Instant coffee would do, and not boiling hot. She wanted him gone as quickly as possible. When she carried the tray back, she wasn't at all pleased to see that only one lamp had been left alight and Patrick was stretched full-length along the couch, fast asleep. If he thought he was staying he could think again. With a sigh she set the tray down on the coffee-table and bent over to wake him up, only to find herself suddenly seized by a pair of amazingly strong arms which pulled her down and around so swiftly that her yelp of shock was still unvoiced as she wound up trapped by Patrick's body and the back of the couch.

Shock quickly gave way to irritation, and she pushed at his shoulders. 'Let me up. Stop playing the fool!' she said testily, too tired to find him amusing.

Patrick grinned, and the look in his eyes was much more intent and purposeful. 'Isn't this much more comfortable?'

Leigh refused to panic as she discovered he was far stronger than she expected him to be, and her attempts to push him off were easily thwarted, but her heart gave a kick against her chest. 'No,' she declared emphatically, 'it is not.'

Patrick lowered his head to her neck, pressing moist kisses upwards until his teeth closed on her earlobe. 'Relax, darling, let yourself go.'

'Get off me, Patrick! I'm not in the mood for your jokes!' she commanded forcefully. 'I mean it. Right now!'

He chuckled. 'Ah, come on, Leigh, you know you don't mean that,' he urged and brought his mouth down on hers, kissing her hungrily, his tongue forcing its way inside her mouth, making her gag.

It suddenly dawned on Leigh that he was serious. It had to be the drink that was making him force himself on her like this, for usually he took her rejection in good part. The knowledge scarcely helped. Shocked, she tore her mouth away. Breathlessly she tried to get his attention, but he was deaf to her angry words. Instead his lips continued to plunder their way down her throat. She tried to jerk free, but his body was a dead weight, and she began to know real fear. She felt the straps of her dress part as she struggled, and when his lips found her breast she let out a piercing scream.

He didn't even falter in his intent for a second. Never had she expected Patrick to attack her like this, and anger and shock gave way to a primitive panic. As his mouth found hers again she made frantic efforts to fight him off, but his strength sapped hers. He was immovable, and nausea rose in her throat as she realised she was no match for him.

Her brain was screaming the 'No!' she couldn't voice when light exploded around them and Patrick was hauled off her and thrown to the floor. She scarcely heard the altercation that followed. Shuddering and sobbing in relief, she tried to piece her dress together with trembling hands. She couldn't, and, overcome, she curled up into a protective ball and covered her face with her hands.

Her mind totally filled by the horror of the attack, she hardly registered the silence that had fallen.

When the cushions sank beside her, she flinched, until she heard Morgan's voice saying her name softly. 'Leigh? Come on now, honey, he's gone. I'm going to take you upstairs.'

She turned her head, eyes emerald pools of shock that overflowed as she saw the rigid set of his beloved face. 'Morgan! Oh, God!' Her cry was pained as she turned to him and was gathered up into his arms. She clung to him wildly as he stood and carried her from the room and up the stairs to her bedroom.

He laid her on top of her bed, removing her arms from around his neck where she still clung on, not wanting to let go of the security she found in his arms.

'I'll only be a moment,' he told her gruffly, and disappeared. When he came back he lifted her shaking figure and held a glass to her lips.

'Here, drink this,' he ordered in a voice that meant to be obeyed. She did so blindly, though her teeth made staccato noises on the glass, and she choked on the fiery liquid. But it began almost at once to restore the warmth to her body, and abated the dreadful shaking of her limbs.

When he took the glass away, she looked up at his stern face and tears sprang to her eyes. 'Oh, Morgan, thank God you were here! He wouldn't stop!'

'What the hell did you let him in for, you little fool, if you didn't mean to go through with it?' He sighed in angry exasperation.

Leigh shuddered. 'It wasn't ... like that! He'd ... had too much to drink...I...offered him coffee...that was all.' Her voice broke on the memory. 'He grabbed me and ... Oh, God! It was horrible!'

With a viciously muttered expletive, Morgan pulled her into his arms, 'Christ! Don't you know how dangerous it is to lead a man on? Especially one like Healey. I'm surprised something like this hasn't happened before!'

Her breath caught in her throat, and she pushed herself away a little to stare up at him. 'That's a... horrible thing to say! I'm not a tease! I don't lead men on!' she cried forcefully, the tears melting away.

A nerve ticked beside Morgan's mouth as he watched her. 'You're a walking invitation, don't you know that?' he argued harshly.

Her eyes said that couldn't be true, and met implacable blue ones. She shrivelled a little inside, self-doubt clouding her already anguished features. 'Was it my fault, then?' she asked in a shaken whisper.

'For God's sake!' Morgan pulled her resisting figure back into his arms. 'I didn't say you were a walking invitation to rape! You're a beautiful young woman and men are attracted to you. Sooner or later one of them was bound to lose his head. However, there was no excuse for what he tried to do to you, drunk or not.'

She shuddered again. 'I thought you were out, with her. I thought...' She couldn't go on.

'I took Carole home hours ago. I'd been working in the studio. Fortunately for you, I heard you scream as I came in. I'm just glad I arrived in time.'

He couldn't be more glad than she was. She didn't think she would ever forget what had happened tonight. 'Oh, Morgan, I just feel so... dirty,' she said with deep loathing. Betrayed, too, for she had thought Patrick was her friend. She could never see him that way again.

His hand stroked soothingly over her tangled hair. 'A shower will soon make you feel better. Why don't you get your night things together while I go and run the water?' he suggested.

The idea of a shower was wonderful. She wanted to wash away the touch of Patrick's lips and hands—from her mind as well as her body. 'Thanks,' she said, sitting up at last. 'I'd like that.' Only then did she really notice the state of her dress. The bodice was so torn, she might as well have been naked! The flush that suffused her cheeks was painful. 'Oh, God!'

Gentle fingers tipped her head up until she couldn't avoid looking at him. 'Nothing happened,' Morgan told her firmly. 'Just remember that. As for my seeing you, I need hardly say that yours isn't the first woman's body I've seen.'

She found little comfort in the thought. The jealousy she had recognised earlier flared faintly to life. She didn't want to think of all the other women he had known. Nor did she want to hear that seeing her virtually naked didn't affect him at all. She wanted . . . If only she knew. If only she could understand what was going on inside her. Yet she had enough sense to know that all reactions, in the circumstances, were extreme, and she shook her head, calling herself a fool.

Morgan rose and disappeared into her bathroom. Wearily Leigh climbed to her feet and collected her robe and nightdress. As soon as he emerged, she went in. The dress she took off went straight into the bin. Even if it had been in a usable condition, she would never have worn it again. Standing under the spray, she scrubbed her skin until she was pink and raw. Only when she felt really clean did she climb out and reach for the large fluffy towel to pat herself dry. With her nightdress on and her robe, she felt more herself at last, and ventured back into the bedroom.

Morgan was standing by the window, back ramrod straight as he peered out into the night. He seemed miles away, but when she flicked off the bathroom light he looked round. His eyes roved over her swiftly, but their expression was hooded, and she had no idea what he was thinking.

'Feeling better?' The question was cool, almost perfunctory.

Nodding, Leigh bit her lip. He had been so understanding it hurt to feel him distancing himself again. It brought weak tears to her eyes, making her irritable with herself. To hide her emotional reaction, she crossed quickly to the bed, discarding her robe, to climb in and pull the covers up to her chin. She looked at him over them.

'Thank you for coming to my rescue.' She tried to make it light but the last word wavered revealingly.

'I wasn't about to walk past when it sounded as if you were being murdered,' he declared drily, following her lead.

Leigh managed a faint smile, then sobered quickly as a thought occurred to her. 'Did you ... hit him?'

Morgan pulled a wry face and rubbed a hand around his neck. 'I expect I would have if he hadn't been running too fast for me to catch him.'

'Oh!' She met his eyes and found them smiling.

'Precisely. Some of tonight's events had the essence of farce about them. I suggest you try to forget the others. Is there anything else you need?'

An answer was emblazoned on her brain—only you. I've only ever needed you, Morgan. The revealing words were so simple it was startling, and she couldn't utter a word. He took that as answer enough and crossed to the door.

'Try and sleep. Goodnight, Leigh.'

He was being kind, and she wished he weren't so far away, in spirit not body, because she needed him. Yet if she asked him to stay, he wouldn't understand. How could he, when she didn't? 'Goodnight, Morgan, and thank you,' she said softly as he closed the door behind him.

Alone, she lay back and stared up at the ceiling, brain struggling through an emotional maze. Forgetting wasn't easy. If Morgan hadn't been home ... But he had been, and that was what counted. Nothing had happened, except she had received a very nasty shock. Her lids dropped as she could no longer hold them open. She was so tired! But she couldn't sleep for there was something else, something she had discovered—about Morgan.

She fell asleep still struggling with it. At first the effects of the shock and the brandy knocked her out, but soon her sleep became troubled, and she moved restlessly as the events of the night invaded her dreams and were relived in vivid Technicolor. Her own scream woke her in the end, and she found herself sitting up, shivering as her perspiration-soaked body met the cool night air. Shuddering, she dropped her head in her hands.

That was how Morgan found her when he hurried in moments later, clad only in a pair of black pyjama bottoms.

Sitting down on the edge of the bed, he drew her still shaking figure into his arms, and she burrowed against his warm flesh instinctively. 'What was it? A nightmare?'

'Yes,' she agreed, but already the demons were retreating, banished by the strength and reality of the man who held her. 'I didn't mean to scream. I'm sorry I woke you,' she added, sounding breathless to her own ears. Her hands had discovered the silken planes of his back and were sending dizzying signals back along her nerve-ends. Each breath she took was filled with the heady male scent of him. It seemed infinitely cruel that the only chance to be close to him was in moments like this. Her heart ached.

She knew him and yet she didn't know him—or herself. He made her feel such conflicting emotions. Hurt and confusion—anger. Yet she wanted him. Wanted him with a passionate intensity that made every nerve in her body scream. Morgan. Why was it that that one word seemed to hold most of her past and all of her future? She felt as if she held all the pieces of a jigsaw, and yet she couldn't fit them together. But if she could, what would the final picture be?

'You didn't wake me.' Morgan's scratchy voice brought her back to the real world. 'I was only dozing. I was rather expecting something like this.'

'Is that why you're wearing pyjamas?' The inanity of the question made her wince. It unwittingly revealed her knowledge that he normally slept in the raw, and brought to their situation something vastly more intimate, which was the opposite of what she had intended.

Morgan went still. 'Got it in one. I thought it would be better to have some clothes on if I had to come on the run. I didn't want to add to your nightmares.'

'You wouldn't do that,' she said huskily, trying to retrieve the situation, but only making it worse. She found herself eased away until he could see her.

'Really? Isn't that rather a provocative statement to make in the circumstances?' he mocked softly.

Colour flooded her cheeks, 'I didn't mean…oh, forget it!'

'No, I don't think I want to,' he said with an angry laugh. 'Tell me what you meant, Leigh, if it wasn't that seeing me naked wouldn't faze you,' Morgan insisted, eyes agleam.

He took her breath away. He couldn't possibly think she was trying to proposition him after what had happened! She answered doggedly, 'I simply meant that you wouldn't be capable of acting like Patrick.'

'All men are capable of it, if pushed far enough,' he stated with harsh honesty.

'Not you, Morgan,' she disagreed with the utmost conviction, and he gave an odd sort of laugh.

'Thanks for the vote of confidence,' he said gruffly, and their eyes became locked.

For an instant that awareness was there, filling the air with its electrifying charge, and she had to lower her lashes for fear of revealing too much. He eased her away from him and back against the pillows.

'Are you feeling better now?'

Why was it that she should suddenly feel so bereft, so abandoned? Knowing how he regarded her, she was crazy to want to stay in his arms, yet she did. 'Yes,' she admitted huskily.

'Then I'd better go,' he said, and made to get up.

'Must you?' It was only the thought of being left alone again in the darkness with her thoughts that prompted the swift query—or so she told herself.

Morgan shot her a considering look through suddenly narrowed eyes. 'What does that mean?'

His suspicion of her motives made her heart contract. 'I'm scared the nightmare will come back. Please, I don't want to be alone. Couldn't you stay for just a little longer? I know if you do I'll be all right.' Her eyes pleaded with him.

She didn't really expect him to agree, and she was resigning herself to it when he sighed in a curiously defeated way and sat back down again, making himself comfortable against the headboard, legs on top of the covers.

He muttered something which sounded very much like, 'I hope I don't regret this,' then went on more audibly, 'Turn the light out and go to sleep.'

Leigh didn't mind his brusqueness. Just to have him beside her was a comfort she hadn't expected. She allowed herself to relax. It was good to be close. That shimmering sexual awareness was dimmed, leaving only a profound pleasure. In no time at all she was drifting into a dreamless sleep.

The next time Leigh awoke, it was daylight. Laying there in a pool of sunlight, she was aware of a wonderful sense of security and warmth. A smile curved her lips as she made to stretch and found out she couldn't. Her eyes shot open, and looked straight into Morgan's sleeping face, the growth of beard blue-black on his chin.

An instant of surprise was soon dispelled by returning memory, and that comforting feeling she had awoken to was explained. Some time during the night, half sleeping, Morgan must have slipped beneath the covers for warmth, and that was how she had ended up with her head cradled on his bare shoulder, his arm holding her close to his side.

She didn't move, scarcely daring to breathe lest she destroy this perfection. She knew, deep inside, that this was how she always wanted to wake to a new day—in Morgan's arms. Oh, it was crazy, but it felt so right, so safe and secure. Gently she rubbed her cheek against him. If only...

The revealing chain of thought was broken as he stirred, disturbed by her movements. His eyes opened and locked with hers—a beautiful blue that seemed to reach down into her soul for an aeon. Then he frowned, and she saw realisation dawn as he studied his surroundings. She held her breath.

What he might have said then she would never know, for they both heard the approach of footsteps at the same time. There was no time to move, they could only turn as one to stare at the door as, after one brief knock, it opened. Ralph's voice preceded his entrance.

'Good lord, Leigh, it's almost ten o'clock. What's the matter? Are you ill?'

He took two paces into the room and stopped as if he had hit an invisible wall. The silence was awesome as all three stared at each other. It was a tableau that Leigh would never forget.

CHAPTER FIVE

IT WAS Ralph who found his voice first, his face pale and drawn into lines of anger. Not looking at Leigh, he fixed his attention rigidly on his son.

'I'll see you downstairs, in the study, in five minutes,' he snapped curtly, and left the room immediately.

Leigh was thrust roughly aside as Morgan sat up abruptly. White as the sheet that covered them, Leigh scrambled up too.

'Oh, God, what must he be thinking?' she cried, her throat tight with anguish. 'He looked so hurt.' She didn't think she would ever forget that look, and she pressed trembling hands to her cheeks.

Thrusting back the covers, Morgan swung his feet to the floor. 'Do you think I'm blind?' he bit out harshly.

Leigh came up on her knees, distraught that she should be the cause of any pain. 'It's all my fault! I asked you to stay. But how could we know he'd come in and jump to conclusions? Oh, poor Ralph! You'll have to tell him the truth, Morgan.'

He afforded her a scathing look on his way to the door. 'I fully intend to. I don't want him thinking I've seduced his little ewe-lamb.'

He departed on that caustic note, leaving Leigh flooded with guilt. If she had got up as soon as she woke, this would never have happened. It was like a nightmare, only worse, because this was actually happening. She knew she couldn't sit waiting; she had to know what was going on down there. Stomach churning away, she scrambled from the bed and into the first things that came to hand: a pair of jeans and a T-shirt. Slipping moccasins on her feet, she quickly ran a brush through her hair before hurrying downstairs.

At least they weren't shouting, she knew that much from the silence, but as she approached the study door she could hear the rise and fall of their voices, although the actual words themselves were indistinguishable. Unable to go in, she paced up and down outside, coming to a halt abruptly as the door opened with an angry movement and Morgan emerged. She stared at him, eyebrows raised, and he looked at her so angrily, yet so coldly, that her stomach knotted.

She swallowed. 'Well?'

Morgan's jaw was so tightly clenched it looked white. Unspeaking, he shut the door and crossed the hall in long, emotive strides. After a brief hesitation, Leigh followed him into the sitting-room and watched tensely as he poured himself a stiff whisky and drank it straight off.

Her heart sank at the sight. She knew in her bones that, whatever had happened, it wasn't good. 'What did he say?'

Morgan stiffened at the sound of her voice, spine going rigid. It spoke volumes as he turned slowly to face her. 'Brace yourself, darling—we're getting married.'

Leigh's gasp of shock was audible. 'What?' She couldn't accept it. It had to be part of some morbid joke. 'That's crazy! You know we can't.' She advanced on him, unnerved by the frozen anger in his face. 'What did you tell him?'

Morgan's lips twisted bitterly. 'That you and I had discovered we loved each other, of course.'

The colour drained from her cheeks, making her stricken eyes loom large. 'Why?' she croaked in a whisper.

'Why?' he echoed grimly, jaw flexing as he relived that interview. 'Because I found myself cast in the role of vile seducer of innocent youth, and I didn't like it, that's why. My God! My own father was looking at me as if I were a rapist!'

She flinched, feeling his hurt, but all the same...
'Wasn't there any other way? You can't want to marry
me,' she finished on a painful note.

'I'm glad you realise it,' Morgan shot back harshly.
'And no, there wasn't any other way. We both know my
father well enough to know when it's pointless to argue.
There was only one way to make things right, and, as
soon as he gave me the chance to speak, I took it. I value
my father's good opinion of me too much to lose it over
you.'

Leigh closed her eyes at that, swallowing back her own
hurt. 'Did he believe you?'

'Just as quickly as you expected him to.'

Her eyes shot open, chest feeling tight. 'What does
that mean?'

Morgan turned and poured himself another drink. 'It
means I don't like being trapped into anything,' he explained curtly.

'Trapped?' Oh, no! Leigh caught his arm and half
turned him round again. '*I* haven't trapped you,
Morgan,' she declared firmly.

Morgan gave a dry, unamused laugh. 'Haven't you?'

Angry colour stole back into her cheeks. 'You know
I haven't.'

'Then what was last night's little drama all about? Stay
with me, Morgan. I'm frightened, Morgan. I'll be all
right if you're there, Morgan,' he mimicked unkindly.

Leigh was choked. 'You know why I was scared. How
can you say that?'

Bleak eyes regarded her, totally unmoved by her distress. 'Because it's belatedly occurring to me that last
night's attack might have been very neatly set up. Were
you really in any danger, Leigh, or were you playing one
of your mother's tricks? After all, Toby had dropped
you, and Healey would have been doubtful. You have
expensive tastes, so you need someone. It wouldn't have
taken you long to look closer to home for a ready cash
supply.'

She couldn't believe that anything could hurt that much. Her eyes reflected her pain as she removed her hand and awkwardly moved away. 'I see,' she said huskily. 'I had no idea your opinion of me was quite that low. I suppose it would be useless for me to try and defend myself.' Her pride made her lift her chin in spite of the battering it had received. 'Well, don't worry, Morgan, you won't have to marry me. I'll make sure of that.'

She left the room, more hurt and angry than ever before. Marriage to Morgan! It would be like the condemned prisoner putting the hangman's rope around his own neck. Ralph couldn't know what he was doing.

Outside the study door she paused, gathering her composure for an interview that was bound to be difficult. Squaring her shoulders, she knocked and went in. Ralph was standing at the open french window, staring out pensively. He turned slowly to face her, and Leigh was dismayed to see that very little colour had returned to his cheeks. Still, he came round his desk and held out his hands to her.

She went into them at once. 'Oh, Ralph, I'm sorry!' she whispered, choked.

He patted her shoulder soothingly. 'I'm the one who should be sorry. I was young once, too, you know. I didn't mean to embarrass you.'

This was her opportunity and she swallowed to moisten a dry throat. 'Ralph, Morgan and I——'

He interrupted her with a small laugh. 'I know. I must be getting old to forget that sparks don't always come from anger. Of course, I always hoped you'd make a match of it, but when you pooh-poohed the idea I didn't think to argue. When I saw you, I was upset because I thought Morgan was playing fast and loose with you, but he tells me you're getting married, and I couldn't be more delighted.'

Leigh felt as if she were drowning. 'Ralph, please listen to me,' she said quickly, only to be stopped once more as her stepfather's face contorted into lines of pain and he pressed a hand to his chest. 'Ralph!' Fear was a lump of ice in her stomach.

Ralph released her and went to his desk. Sitting down, he took a tablet from a bottle in the drawer and slipped it under his tongue. Within minutes she saw his colour start to come back. He gave her a weak smile.

'I'm sorry, my dear, I didn't mean to alarm you. It's just my angina. Be right as rain in a minute or two. I'm supposed to avoid stressful situations, and this morning was a bit of a shock.' He took a sip of water from a glass on his desk. 'Now, what was it you were going to say?'

The waters closed over her. She hadn't realised Ralph was ill. They had been the cause of one shock already today, and she had seen the result. She simply couldn't add to his stress.

She produced a smile, albeit wavery. 'Nothing. Just that I'm sorry we upset you.'

He chuckled. 'Serves me right for coming home early. Now, you'd better run along back to Morgan. I expect you'll have a lot to talk about.'

What an understatement. 'Yes, I guess we will. Are you sure you're all right? Should I call Dr Radcliffe?'

'That old fusspot? No, no, I'll be quite all right. I'll probably take a nap. Now I won't have you worrying, Leigh, not when you've an engagement to celebrate. So, off you go.'

Leigh slowly returned to the sitting-room, feeling helpless. Morgan was still there, and she sat down heavily on the couch opposite. Looking across, she met his sardonically enquiring blue gaze. Edgily her fingers picked at the arm rest. 'He wouldn't listen,' she stated unnecessarily. 'He seems to think the idea's marvellous.'

'I know,' Morgan grated harshly. 'So you said nothing?' It wasn't really a question, and his look said he hadn't seriously expected her to.

'How could I? He's not well, Morgan.'

'Why do you think I didn't try harder?' he agreed tiredly. 'He's had a bad heart for years. We gave him a shock he didn't need.'

Leigh drew her legs up, circling them with her arms, and resting her chin on her knees. 'What are we going to do?'

Morgan's face became set. 'We go through with it.'

A hammer seemed to hit her chest and she swallowed. 'I can't.'

Angrily he sat forward. 'You can and you damn well will. You got us into this, remember. So we play like a pair of lovers for his benefit and we get married. As soon as possible after that, we get divorced, understood?'

Leigh flinched and lowered her lids to shield her despair from him. 'Yes, I understand.' What else could they do? But how on earth was she going to survive it? She had the feeling it would destroy her...unless... Looking at him, she bit her lip uncertainly.

Seeing it, Morgan's eyes narrowed. 'What the hell's going through that mind of yours now?' he asked in sharp suspicion.

The chasm that had opened between them seemed to be growing wider. Couldn't he see that they had to try and bridge it somehow if life together was to be halfway tolerable? Licking dry lips, she said softly, 'I was only thinking that, if we have to get married, we could try and make a go of it, Morgan.'

He looked as if he had been waiting for her to say just that. 'Oh, no! That's not on, sweetheart. I thought that was all part of your tawdry little plan. Well, you won't have me jumping through hoops the way your mother did with my father. We get married to please the old man, and divorced to please me. In between—nothing. Is that clear? Don't go thinking this is going to be a real marriage, because it isn't!'

Leigh looked away. Her heart ached, but she wasn't going to let him see how his coldness could hurt her. 'I only thought——'

'I know what you only thought, but I'll tell you how it will be,' he interrupted brusquely. 'In company we pretend to be lovers, but that all stops the second we're alone. It doesn't get me into your bed again.'

That brought her to her feet, unable to take any more. 'I haven't invited you there!' she rejoined angrily. 'And as this wedding is a sham, we'd better not compound it by having a church wedding. I'll tell Ralph we've decided on a civil ceremony. We don't want any romantic hypocrisy, do we?'

Morgan smiled thinly. 'Now you're getting the picture. The sooner we get the farce over with, the better!'

Farce! It was going to be more like a tragedy in three acts, Leigh thought, feeling as if she were being shredded. 'What now? I take it you do have a plan?' She used sarcasm as a weapon to hide behind.

'Now, I'm going to work. The fun begins tonight. If we're going to be convincing, we'll have to spend time together. We'll go out to dinner. I'll meet you in the hall at eight.'

Leigh had no option but to agree and watch him walk away. The situation was impossible. If there ever had been a chance to win his respect, it was lost forever now. A dry laugh broke from her. Hadn't she got over that yet? Wasn't she ever going to learn? It seemed not, and she couldn't understand why. Only a fool would continually put themselves in the firing line. She was turning out to be the biggest fool she knew.

She went down to meet him that evening, feeling as if all the joy had gone out of her. She had spent a lot of time and energy on her appearance to cover up her inner misery. The black and blue satin dress had been an unconscious choice. The colours suited her, adding a fragility to her face. It was entirely coincidental that they reflected her mood. She had piled her hair up, because that always seemed to give her more confidence, and the careful use of make-up had turned her eyes into huge green pools of mystery.

Morgan was waiting for her, looking breathtakingly handsome in a dark dinner suit and white silk dress shirt. Her fingers tensed about her purse as she joined him, waiting for an acid comment.

However, none was forthcoming. He simply said, 'We'd better say goodbye to Dad before we go.'

Ralph was listening to a radio play, but looked up with a smile as they appeared beside him. 'All set? You look marvellous, Leigh. You're a very lucky man, son. Well, don't let me keep you. Enjoy yourselves, and don't make too much noise when you come in. An old man like me needs his sleep.'

Leigh bent to kiss his cheek, producing a smile that would allay any doubts he might have. 'You're not old, you just like getting sympathy.'

He laughed and waved them off.

Morgan had booked a table at a restaurant some miles away. It wasn't a place she had ever been to before, but she was glad of the anonymity, for it would mean they would be unlikely to run into anyone they knew. He had barely spoken during the drive, but Leigh hadn't seen anything unusual in that. When the silence continued long after their meal had been served, she knew it was a deliberate ploy. Quite what he hoped to achieve she didn't know, but if it was to annoy her he succeeded.

She bore it as long as she could, then set her knife and fork down with a sigh. 'Am I being sent to Coventry, or have you suddenly taken a vow of silence?'

Morgan glanced across at her. 'Neither. I may be forced to marry you, but keeping you entertained wasn't part of the deal.''

His attitude was infuriating. He had no right to push all the blame on to her. 'It works two ways, you know. Surely the least we can do is be polite to each other.'

His jaw tensed. 'Right now, being polite is beyond me, sweetheart. I still feel bloody murderous. So I suggest you concentrate on your dinner and forget any thoughts of idle chit-chat.'

The thought of food made her stomach churn. 'I'm trapped too, remember? It's no picnic for me either.'

A mocking smile twisted his lips. 'Things not going quite the way you planned? Poor Leigh. My heart bleeds for you.'

She was forced to look away from the taunt in his eyes. 'Shut up!' she ordered through clenched teeth.

'Gladly,' he retorted smartly and returned to his dinner.

She watched him in silence for a moment, wishing she could leave. 'How long must we stay here?' The question broke from her, sounding far too desperate.

'Long enough so that Dad doesn't suspect anything's wrong. If you don't like it, just remember, you made the bed.'

She relapsed gratefully into silence after that, merely pecking at her food, willing the time to pass. Morgan was enjoying her discomfort, and she hated that. Her palm itched to wipe the curl from his lips—and she guessed he probably knew that, too. Not surprisingly, the tension brought on a headache that dulled her eyes and drew lines beside her mouth. If this was how their marriage was going to be, she wouldn't be able to bear it.

They left at eleven, by which time Leigh had had more than enough. Her head was throbbing, and the rest of her felt as if she'd gone through the mill. The house was dark when they reached it, and she was glad. She wouldn't have been able to fool anyone tonight, least of all Ralph. She went straight to her room, the strength leaving her as she closed the door. She had to bite down hard on her lip to keep weak tears at bay. He wasn't going to make her cry.

Wearily she showered and got ready for bed, taking two aspirin for her headache. Still she couldn't sleep as a result of it, but lay looking up at the ceiling dry-eyed until the sky began to lighten outside. It was going to be another lovely day, but in her heart it was raining.

It was still very early when she rose and changed into jeans and a thick jumper, and, carrying her riding boots for fear of waking anyone, slipped quietly down the stairs and let herself out of the house. It didn't take long to get to the stables and saddle up the willing mare, and for the next couple of hours Leigh left her worries behind. The remnants of her headache disappeared as she revelled in her freedom. But everything had to end some time and eventually she had to turn the horse round and head for home. She spent as long as she could grooming Bones, then made her way back up to the house.

Head lowered, lost in thought, she didn't see Ralph taking his coffee on the terrace until he spoke.

'You're up with the lark, Leigh.'

She looked up with a start, smiling faintly because, in a changing world, he was reassuringly familiar. 'I couldn't sleep. I took Bones out instead,' she explained as she mounted the steps and walked round to the table, stooping to kiss his cheek. 'Is there any more coffee?'

Ralph waved a hand. 'Help yourself.'

She did and perched herself on the coping to drink it, staring pensively out over the lawn to the copse.

'You look sad.' Ralph's observation broke in on her thoughts, making her jump.

She looked round, valiantly smiling. 'Do I? I was just thinking how, soon, everything would change.'

'Because you're marrying my son? That makes you sad?' The question was gentle but the eyes were keen.

Leigh looked down into her cup. 'Marriage is a big step,' she said gravely, the awkwardness of her position never more apparent.

'And you're not sure if you're doing the right thing?' he prompted.

She raised a diffident shoulder. 'Something like that.'

Ralph put aside his cup and came to sit on the wall facing her, expression serious. 'Leigh, my dear, if anything's wrong you can tell me. Yesterday you seemed so happy. I thought you loved Morgan?'

Loved Morgan. The words seemed to echo in her mind and in her heart. *Loved Morgan.* Her gaze remained fixed on the beautiful gardens as, kaleidoscopically, the pieces of the jigsaw fell into place and the true picture was revealed to her at last. She loved him. Not, as she had thought, the way she used to as a child, but as a woman. She must have been blind not to see it. Down in the copse Morgan had kissed her for the first time. She should have realised then that she loved him. All the signs had been there.

Everything made sense. All her confusion and anger. Without realising it, she had fallen fathoms deep in love with him. So deep, there was no escape. Her heart had known he was perfect for her—the very reason for her existence. Only her mind had still seen him through the eyes of a child. Then she had thought that marriage was a dreadful mistake. Now she knew that to be Morgan's wife was something she longed for above all else. Life without him...it was unthinkable.

The cup shook in its saucer and she quickly put both down. She kept her head lowered. 'I love him more than life itself,' she confessed passionately, then looked at her stepfather, eyes wide and honest. 'I've loved him all my life, but this is different. I...can't imagine a life without him. He's all I'll ever want. I've been awfully blind, but he's been like a brother so long I never thought I'd marry him.'

Ralph smiled, moved by the passion in her voice. 'Now you are. So why the long face?'

Because I know the man I love despises me. Feels only contempt. That was the truth she could never tell him, now more than ever. She swallowed a lump that rose to choke her, and tried to shrug. 'I know, I'm being foolish.' Somehow she had to find a suitable lie and make it convincing. It wasn't hard. The answer was in her aching heart. 'It frightens me. I love him, but I don't think it will be enough!'

He didn't try to make light of it. 'There are no guarantees, my dear. Just always remember you love him, and show him that love. Be yourself. That's who he fell in love with.'

Leigh scarcely knew whether to laugh or cry. 'I know. I'm just being ridiculous.'

'No, you're not,' he contradicted, patting her knee. 'You're just being like anyone who's ever been in love since time began. It's the most wonderful, and, at the same time, most unnerving emotion known to man.'

For his sake she dredged up a smile. 'I won't argue with that. I can make him happy, Ralph, given the chance.' A chance Morgan would never allow her.

'What more can a man ask for?'

'What indeed?' Her smile hid the bitterness that lay behind the words. She cursed the fate that could deal her such a crippling blow. She rose to her feet before he could say anything more. 'I'd better go and shower. I smell of horse.' More, she needed time alone, to think. To erect defences that would stop Morgan ever knowing how she felt.

'By the way, Leigh,' Ralph's voice halted her departure. 'I telephoned your mother last night. She'll be here some time this afternoon.' He sounded apologetic.

She smiled wryly, accepting that it had been inevitable even if it was the very last thing she wanted. Unlike Ralph, Una never took anything at face-value. There was nothing she liked better than intrigue, and she could smell one a mile off. Pretending to her was going to be something entirely different.

Full of inevitably gloomy thoughts at the prospect, Leigh rounded the corner of the terrace and walked slap-bang into the solid figure who had planted himself in her path.

'Oh!' Her gasp of alarm died as she looked up into Morgan's icily mocking blue eyes.

'Well, well, well,' he murmured lazily. 'If it isn't my unknown admirer!'

Leigh felt as if every function in her body had stopped. She went white. 'You heard.' The flat statement left numb lips.

His teeth flashed. 'Every interesting word.' He stared down into her stricken face curiously. 'Do you really love me, Leigh?' he queried softly.

Her heart turned over. He was playing with her. She knew he was playing with her, and the cruelty of it brought a wave of anger sweeping over her. He was taunting her with the fact that it was all an act, and she had had enough. In that moment her hatred was as strong as her love and both overrode caution. It drove her on to do the thing he least expected. To tell the truth and shame the devil. 'Yes,' she admitted huskily, 'I do love you, Morgan.' The eyes she raised to his were a deep, smoky emerald. Of course, the second it was done, she regretted it, but it was much too late to retreat. Pride alone kept her rooted to the spot.

Morgan simply stared at her for a moment or two, then threw back his head and laughed. Scalding tears burned the back of her eyes but she wouldn't let them fall. Her nails scored arcs into her hands as she made herself stay where she was and take his mockery even as pain lanced through her. He wouldn't make her cry, neither would she run away.

He subsided finally and eyed her rigid figure in sardonic amusement. 'Love?' he scorned. 'Neither you nor your mother know what love is. Not the selfless sort.'

'You're wrong,' she argued in a taut voice. 'Just as you've been wrong about me for months.'

His lips curled. 'Am I? Or is it you? Lust isn't love, darling.'

Hot colour stained her cheeks. 'I know that.'

'Do you? I've never seen love from you.'

Steadfastly she held his eyes. 'Then *you* don't know love, because that's *all* you've ever had from me, Morgan. I'd like to hate you now, but I can't. I didn't ask to love you, I had no choice.'

There must have been some quality in her eyes or voice, perhaps both, that made him stop mocking and actually look at her. His eyes narrowed. 'My God, you actually believe what you're saying,' he declared incredulously.

At last she had his attention! 'There's no point in lying,' she answered him simply, because it was far too late for that.

Morgan shook his head. 'Disregarding the fact that I don't believe a word of it, don't you realise how crazy that is?'

Almost, she laughed. 'To love someone who doesn't love me, who would never allow himself to fall in love with me? Yes, I know. That must make me as blind as you, for I do love you.'

'This is absurd!'

At last they agreed on something! She lifted her chin proudly. 'Isn't it?'

Morgan dragged a hand through his hair impatiently. 'Damn you, Leigh Armstrong, I don't want you to love me!' he declared furiously.

His anger made her flinch but she remained firm. 'I'm sorry, Morgan, but I don't know how to not love you.'

'Find a way, for God's sake!' he growled. 'Or I will.'

She began to feel rather hysterical. 'I think it will have to be you, because it's stronger than I am.' She gave a queer sort of laugh. 'You'll have to try and make me hate you, Morgan, really hate you. I don't know if you can do that. You've never succeeded up till now. But who knows, perhaps you'll be lucky? Until you do, you'll just have to accept it, as I have.' With that she brushed past him, taking the back stairs up to her room two at a time.

Inside, with the door safely closed, Leigh flung herself on to her bed, fingers curling into the fluffy counterpane. What had she done? Given him a rod to beat her with, that was what she had done! She had burnt her boats beyond hope of salvage and now she couldn't start pretending not to care. All she could do now was be true to herself, whatever the pain it brought her. Morgan might not want her love, refusing to believe any such emotion could exist, yet she'd make him accept that she believed it. If she tried denying her feelings, he'd say she had been lying all the time. Which left only one road to take. She must show him her love and risk his mockery and rejection.

Her love would survive it. She might have invited him to destroy it, but deep inside she knew that was impossible. She was like a plant, starved and neglected of the staff of life, and yet stubbornly refusing to die.

From now on it was going to get worse, but she'd show him what she was made of. She wasn't going to deny the most important part of herself. She loved him and he'd have to accept it. She wasn't her mother, and she'd prove that too. One of them was going to have to break, and it wasn't going to be her.

CHAPTER SIX

UNA arrived, with a mountain of luggage, at teatime. She swept into the house in a cloud of Ysatis, a tall, elegant, still beautiful woman. Today she was in a powder-blue two-piece that Leigh was pretty sure she could put a name to. If appearances said anything, her mother was prospering. She barely paused long enough to greet her husband before whisking her daughter off for a quiet tête-à-tête over tea.

'What on earth have you been up to, darling?' she asked in sly amusement. It had been a sad day when she'd realised her daughter had inherited nothing from her but her looks. She had always found Leigh's quietness and solemn eyes disagreeably uncomfortable, and had taken to chaffing her as a consequence.

Used to being baited, Leigh handed her mother a cup of tea and responded patiently. 'What exactly do you mean, Mother?'

Una waved an eloquent hand. 'Well, darling, you and Morgan? I was never more stunned than when Ralph telephoned.' Her eyes glittered. 'Are you pregnant?'

Leigh almost laughed, her mother was so predictable. 'No, I'm not pregnant.'

'Then how on earth did you manage to catch him?'

'Is it totally impossible that we should love each other?' Leigh returned in exasperation.

Her mother gave her a quizzical look. 'All right, you don't have to tell me. You always were a secretive child! Anyway, I just never knew you had it in you, darling. You always looked so disapprovingly at me. Still, it's a clever move. Morgan is going to be a very rich man one day. A woman should look to the future.'

'Is that what you were doing when you made a play for Morgan yourself?' Leigh asked squarely.

Una was momentarily taken aback. 'My, you have exchanged secrets, haven't you, darling?' she murmured coolly, sipping at her tea. 'Was that before or after you set your little trap?'

'I'm not that mercenary, Mother.' Leigh refused to get angry, knowing she would be the loser.

Una laughed. 'Don't come that holier-than-thou attitude. You're a woman. You'll do anything you have to to keep the man you want, and you know it.' Setting her cup down, she sat back and crossed one slim leg over the other. 'So, you've fallen in love with Morgan. I suppose I could have predicted that. So the question really is—does he love you?'

Leigh had known that was coming, and that it would be imperative to hold her mother's gaze. 'Of course.'

'Hmm,' Una mused thoughtfully, watching as her daughter returned her cup to the tray.

Leigh set her chin and met the identical green eyes. 'You can always ask him,' she suggested sweetly.

'I may just do that,' her mother agreed, then laughed low down in her throat. 'What *is* he getting into?' she said in barely a whisper, but Leigh heard and her eyes narrowed.

'Mother!' she warned sternly.

'Oh, all right,' Una grimaced. 'But let me give you a piece of advice, darling. I don't think it would be a good idea to go in for a family right away. Children won't hold someone like Morgan.'

Leigh tried unsuccessfully to probe the surface of her mother's face. 'I won't need to *hold* him, as you put it. Mother, what are you up to?'

Una looked hurt. 'Up to? Darling, I'm only thinking of you. If you want to keep him, don't get pregnant. He'll only feel more trapped. You've got to give him plenty of room and plenty of time. He'll come round. Believe me, I know men.'

And that, thought Leigh drily, was the only statement of her mother's she would never think of disputing.

The rest of the conversation preyed on her mind as she dressed for dinner. She had the uneasy sensation that her mother had some plan of her own in mind, though for the life of her she couldn't think what or why. All she knew was that it would pay her to stay on the alert. And that was an irony in itself, worrying about saving her marriage from her mother's interference when it wasn't going to last anyway!

With the revelations of the morning uppermost in her thoughts, Leigh lingered over her make-up. Meeting Morgan again was going to be unnerving, and she decided to defuse the situation by being deliberately late. Yet when she finally descended to the sitting-room for a pre-dinner drink, it was to find only Morgan present. As she hesitated in the doorway, he looked up and caught her standing there. It was impossible, now, to retreat, so she made herself walk into the room under the sardonic appraisal of his vivid blue eyes.

'I thought I was late,' she declared revealingly, checking her watch against the mantel-clock, and striving for a coolness she could never feel in Morgan's company. Especially now. She wished she hadn't decided to wear the simple black cocktail dress with its *diamanté* straps and swirling silver threadwork on the blouson bodice, for his eyes seemed to go right through the thin fabric.

'You are,' he confirmed, rising effortlessly to his feet and sauntering to the cocktail trolley. 'What can I get you?'

'Vodka and tonic, please.' Her eyes followed his movements, noting how well the dinner suit became him, and she experienced a wayward tug of desire that brought colour to her cheeks. How well she remembered those all-too-brief moments in his arms, and wondered if she would ever feel them close about her again. Somehow she doubted it. With a little sigh, she took a seat and cleared her throat. 'Where's Ralph?'

Morgan returned with her drink, handing it to her with elaborate care before sitting down again. 'Your mother waylaid him half an hour ago. They're still in the study. Perhaps you should have taken the possibility into consideration and waited a little longer,' he taunted.

It was typical of him to guess her ploy, but she decided to ignore it. 'What can they be talking about?' So far as she could recall, in recent years Una and Ralph had rarely held a conversation that lasted more than ten minutes.

'At a guess, I'd say the wedding,' Morgan supplied drily.

Oh, lord! 'Ralph has it all arranged,' she protested.

Morgan laughed without amusement. 'By now you can safely bet his plans have been vetoed. Una has no intention of allowing anyone to rain on her parade. As mother of the bride, she'll want her day to shine. You can kiss the idea of a quiet wedding goodbye as of now.'

It was all too horribly probable. Though she hadn't acknowledged it, Leigh had always known that her mother's arrival would turn an already tense situation into near farce.

'I can see why people elope!' she joked wryly.

Morgan raised his brows. 'Are you suggesting we do the same?'

If, loving her, he was to ask her to do that very thing, she would, but he didn't love her, and so... 'No, that's for lovers, and we aren't like them.'

'Disappointed you're being hanged for a sheep when you're still a lamb, Leigh?' Morgan queried ironically.

Just how much of a lamb she was, he would never know. 'Relieved,' she lied blandly. 'That's one situation I'm thankful to avoid.'

'That wasn't the impression I received.'

A dull flush rose in her cheeks as the first of many exchanges slipped through her guard. Well, she had invited him to do his worst, and she hadn't thought he wouldn't try. 'You were hardly disinterested yourself, Morgan. Or do you have a selective memory?'

His smile wasn't kind. 'No, darling, just a healthy male libido.'

Her breath caught and she dropped her eyes to her glass to hide from him the stark pain she knew was there. It was going to be worse than she imagined. He had a thousand ways to hurt her, and she had none. A fine tremor ran across the surface of her drink as she raised the glass to her lips. Over the rim, she met his eyes, and they were glittering in mocking acknowledgement of a hit. Anger raced through her and took charge of her tongue.

'I see. Then you must have wanted my mother, too, before you turned her down! After all, we're alike, you say, so if you wanted me, you must have wanted her.' She laughed. 'My God, and you act so pure! You're a hypocrite, Morgan Fairfax——Oh!' The last words tailed off sharply as he left his seat, hands like a vice on her shoulders, dragging her to her feet. He gave her one almighty shake that snapped her neck painfully and made her drop her glass.

'That's enough!' he barked, beside himself with anger. 'I have never, *never* felt anything for Una but complete contempt! Is that clear?'

Her neck hurt, but that faded under the twin joys of knowing she had got under his skin successfully, and, more important, that he had never wanted her mother. Until that moment she hadn't realised how much she loathed the idea that he might have. Her eyes glowed with a fierce joy, and Morgan saw it.

'My God! You were jealous!'

She didn't bother to deny it, just looked up at him as he gazed down incredulously at her. He was so close, she could smell the fragrance of his cologne and, underlying that, a scent that was far more potent. Desire was a fierce ache inside her, making her want to close the gap between them, to press herself close and feel his lips on hers. Her throat closed over. It had been so long. As she gazed at him helplessly, she saw the birth of an answering desire in his own eyes, and his hands tightened on her flesh, making her wince.

'You're hurting me,' she breathed huskily.

'God!' Morgan thrust her away to turn his back on her.

Her heart contracted. 'Morgan?'

'Shut up!' The order was cast viciously over his shoulder.

Leigh sighed and absently rubbed at her arms. Her emotions were travelling on a switchback that now plummeted her sickeningly. There was no pleasure in hurting him. 'I'm sorry,' she apologised, reaching out a tentative hand to touch his rigid back.

'Don't bother,' he snarled, moving just enough for her hand to fall away. 'You got your pound of flesh.'

Briefly she closed her eyes. 'It wasn't like that,' she protested.

He turned, eyes scathing. 'Wasn't it? You've satisfied yourself that it's you I wanted, still want, and not your mother. But it changes nothing. Wanting doesn't mean having, Leigh. A few months of celibacy won't hurt you, then you can indulge yourself in the Patrick Healeys of this world to your heart's content.'

Leigh paled, cut to the heart. 'Oh, God, that was cruel!'

Morgan gave a harsh bark of laughter. 'You laid down the terms, Leigh. You didn't ask for quarter, so you'll get none,' he declared, eyeing her watchfully.

What was he waiting for, the blood? 'I never expected any. Just remember, one battle isn't the war. As you said, nothing has changed. Nothing.' Her steady gaze underlined her meaning.

They were still staring at each other when Ralph escorted Una into the room only seconds later. One look at the tableau made Una utter a peal of amused laughter.

'Surely to goodness you haven't been arguing already?' she chaffed them, arranging herself gracefully in a corner of the couch. 'I'll have a martini, darling.' She smiled at her husband, and then returned to the newly engaged couple. 'What was it, a lovers' tiff? This won't do at all. Why don't you kiss and make up? Ralph and I will promise not to look,' she went on archly.

It was time, Leigh realised, for their first performance as the happy couple. Giving Una an old-fashioned look, she moved to Morgan's side and slipped her hand through his arm. 'Mother, you're the limit. There's nothing to make up, is there, darling?' It wasn't easy to voice the endearment, and as she tipped her head up to smile at him she saw by the sardonic humour in his eyes that he realised it, and enjoyed her discomfort. All the same, he followed her lead and smiled back down at her. It didn't, she noticed, reach his eyes.

'No, and if there were it would be done in private, not for your amusement, Una,' he responded smoothly.

She laughed in her most sultry fashion. 'I'm sure it will. But really, Morgan, you'll have to start calling me Mother once you're married to Leigh,' Una provoked.

Leigh had never gauged the exact pitch of the tension between Morgan and Una before. Now, ultra-sensitive to the atmosphere, she did. There was an edge to it that wasn't pleasant, and she stiffened slightly, watching them closely.

Morgan was smiling. 'Will I? Are you sure you want to be called Mother by a man my age? How will your image stand it?' Rapier-swift, he ducked under her guard and scored a hit.

Una's smile frayed slightly. 'Now, now, darling, that isn't very nice. A woman doesn't want to be reminded of her age.'

'In that case, I'll call you Una, just as I always have ... Mother.'

Leigh caught her breath, waiting for her mother's anger to erupt at that. Before anything could happen, though, Ralph's calm voice preserved the peace.

'Now, Morgan, don't tease,' he reproved mildly.

Tease? Leigh's mind boggled at that description. Surely he hadn't missed the underlying animosity between his wife and son! It was almost palpable. Yet he made no outward sign as he returned with Una's drink. Handing it to her, he kicked Leigh's fallen glass, and he bent to retrieve it. He glanced sternly at the pair of them.

'What *was* going on in here?'

'I don't see a bruise, so I assume Morgan must have ducked in time,' Una drawled, her voice clearly saying it was a pity.

Leigh threw her an exasperated look. 'I didn't throw it, Mother, I dropped it.'

'But how, darling? Or can I guess? Really, Morgan, you must learn to control your passions. Leigh always did bruise easily.'

Leigh felt Morgan stiffen angrily and hastened into the breach. 'Mother, I love you, but you really are a first-class stirrer! Now stop it, and let's go in to dinner before it gets cold.'

Una gave her a grudging look of respect. 'I do believe my little girl is growing up.'

Her daughter smiled wryly. 'It happens to us all eventually. Even you, Mother.'

Una threw her a look of mock alarm as she rose to her feet. 'God, I hope not!'

Ralph and her mother led the way out. Leigh would have followed but Morgan held her back. She looked up at him enquiringly.

'You don't have to try and shield me from Una's verbal darts; I'm quite capable of looking after myself, you know.'

'I know, but neither of you seem to care about how Ralph feels. Well, I do, and I'm telling you now, Morgan, I won't have it. He deserves better from you both, especially you.'

'What are you trying to do, impress me with the fact that you are a caring person after all?' he scorned.

Leigh drew in her breath. 'Oh, Morgan, sometimes I could cheerfully hit you!'

'I wouldn't suggest you try it.'

'Why not? You wouldn't hit me back.'

He looked amused. 'You can't be sure of that.'

'Oh, but I can. You see, you're Ralph's son, and that makes it impossible,' she said quietly. 'He wouldn't dream of hurting anyone. Not even my mother.'

'Ah! Now I understand. Are you hoping I'll also be as weak as my father and fall for a woman like Una? Preferably yourself? Oh, no, Leigh, that will never happen. I'm neither that weak nor that foolish!'

'Picking the wrong woman doesn't make Ralph weak, Morgan, only human. But at least it shows he had guts enough to love somebody.'

Morgan was furious. 'Are you implying I'm a coward?'

'An emotional one, yes. You're afraid, Morgan. Afraid to trust yourself in case you should prove to have the same failings as the rest of us!' Leigh taunted, knowing by every instinct she possessed that she had hit on the truth.

'Your basis for the argument being that I don't love you? That doesn't mean I can't or don't love somebody else,' he pointed out witheringly.

That was something she had never dreamt of, and suddenly she found herself poised over a dark pit of despair. 'Do you?'

'Poor Leigh,' he jeered softly. 'That really mucks up your plans, doesn't it? Were you banking on my having a secret passion for you? Now you know I don't, do you want to change your mind and not love me after all?'

Choked, she stared up at him. 'Damn you, no.'

'Don't be stubborn. Even Una knows when to give in gracefully.'

She was beginning to hate the very mention of her mother! 'Maybe she does, but obviously I'm not that clever.' If I were I wouldn't let myself love you.

'Then the sooner you wise up, the better for both of us!' he rejoined caustically.

'What's keeping you two?' Ralph's voice interrupted a second or two before he appeared in the doorway. It gave them just enough time to clear all traces of the exchange from their faces. 'I know it's normal to lose your appetite, but some of us around here are hungry.'

'We'll be right with you, Dad,' Morgan responded with a grin, and when Ralph disappeared again he turned narrowed eyes on Leigh. 'I suggest you think long and hard about this ridiculous charade you're playing, darling, starting right now. Whatever you're after, all you're going to get is grief.'

Following him from the room, Leigh knew he was probably right. But what choice did she have? She couldn't say, 'I won't love you because it hurts.' All she could do was bear it as best she could.

Halfway through dinner, Una brought up the subject of the wedding. Setting down her knife and fork, she turned to her daughter.

'Now then, darling, Ralph and I have had a nice long talk, and he's going to have a word with the vicar tomorrow. With three weeks to call the banns, the wedding can be set a month today. I've already informed the Press, so the notices will be in tomorrow's papers. Naturally, the reception will be held here. We'll open up the ballroom and have a marquee on the west lawn in case of rain. You must let me have your guest lists as soon as possible. It's short notice, so the invitations simply must go out immediately.'

Leigh met Morgan's bland expression and the lift of his lips that seemed to say, 'She's your mother,' and realised he was leaving the battle up to her. She wasn't prepared to let him get away with it.

'Mother, Morgan wants a civil ceremony. Isn't that so, darling?' She turned to him, eyebrows raised, for confirmation, smiling as she watched his eyes narrow wrathfully.

'Nonsense!' Una dismissed at once, not giving him a chance to speak. 'My only daughter isn't going to get married in some dingy office. You deserve a white wedding, and you're going to have one. My mind is quite made up.'

Leigh moulded her face into a picture of indecision as she appealed to Morgan once more. 'Darling?'

This time, though, he was ready for her. 'I want what you want, sweetheart,' he responded gallantly, and reached his right hand across to her. After the faintest hesitation, she placed her left hand in his. 'How could I deny you anything?' He sounded sincere, but his eyes mocked her and she paled a little.

'How charming!' Una declared delightedly, but with a faint edge to her voice. 'But what's this? No ring?' She drew all eyes to Leigh's bare hand.

'We're going to buy one this weekend,' Morgan responded smoothly.

'Buy one!' Una exclaimed in astonishment. 'But surely——' She broke off theatrically.

Leigh suppressed a gasp as Morgan's fingers tightened painfully about hers.

'Go on, Una, you can't stop there.' His voice was so controlled, Leigh knew that only she was aware of just how angry he was.

Una addressed herself to Ralph. 'Surely Leigh should have the family ring, darling? Naturally, I never expected to wear it, but it's Leigh's right, as Morgan's fiancée.'

Releasing Leigh's hand, Morgan shot his stepmother an amused look. 'As I recall, you threw a fit over it.'

Leigh watched her mother's colour deepen and made a discovery. She must have been blind not to see it before. Una might react hostilely towards Morgan, but underlying that was desire. Her mother was still attracted to him, and Morgan knew it.

Did Ralph know? One look down the table showed him busy with his dinner. He seemed oblivious, and she hoped he was. She was torn between anger and pity for her mother, but at the same time the hairs on the back of her neck rose. Una was dangerous, and Morgan was a fool to taunt her so blatantly.

Once more she placed herself between them verbally. 'What ring? I didn't know there was one.'

Morgan looked highly sceptical but obliged her by explaining, 'It's a square-cut emerald set with diamonds. Traditionally it's passed down to the wife of the eldest son of the family.'

'Morgan's mother was the last to wear it,' Ralph spoke up, revealing he had been following the conversation. 'Now, of course, it will be yours.'

'So an Armstrong woman will wear it after all,' his son declared, casting Una a look heavy with irony.

Leigh's heart sank to a new low. No wonder Morgan was angry. He believed that she and Una had conspired to get the ring one way or another. Her mother had coveted it, but had been deprived of it on her own marriage. Morgan couldn't refuse her, but it was plain he didn't think her worthy of wearing his mother's ring.

Traditional or not, Leigh knew that unless it was freely given she didn't want it. She shook her head. 'This Armstrong won't. I'd rather have a simple solitaire.'

The silence that followed her statement was swiftly broken.

'Are you mad?' Una exclaimed in horror. 'My God, it's worth a king's ransom. I don't understand you!'

'No, Mother, you never have,' Leigh returned softly. 'The value isn't in the ring. That's just a lump of stone someone dug out of the ground. It's the sentiment that counts. Don't you understand, Mother? A curtain ring would have more value if it was given with love.'

'Elizabeth was proud to wear the ring because I gave it to her, and I'd like to think it brought us happiness,' Ralph said quietly. 'That is what I wish for you and Morgan too. You must allow him to give you the ring, my dear.'

Leigh swallowed a lump in her throat, knowing that nothing could bring her the happiness she craved. 'If Morgan wants me to have the ring, then I shall wear it as proudly as Elizabeth,' she said huskily, and turned to look at him. The coldness in his eyes was the harshest rejection, but she refused to look away, although her cheeks paled.

'I'll get it from the safe after dinner,' he said shortly.

Leigh bent her head over her plate, pretending to eat when really she had no appetite at all.

'Have you decided where you're going for your honeymoon yet?' Una wanted to know next. 'I know someone who has a friend who has a hideaway on Mustique. I could——'

'I doubt if we'll have time for a honeymoon right now, Una,' Morgan interrupted forcibly.

'No honeymoon? I never heard of such a thing,' Una declared in amazement.

'Neither have I.' Ralph added, giving his son a long, hard stare. 'Of course you'll have one, and it shall be my wedding present to you both. I don't want to hear any arguments,' he finished as Morgan made to speak.

Morgan held his father's gaze for a second or two before nodding. 'Very well, Dad. Leigh, if you've finished, we might as well go along to the study now.'

Leigh had had more than enough, of food and her mother's plans. She rose at once and went with him. As soon as the door shut behind them, Una turned to her husband.

'Ralph, I hate to have to say this about your son, but I have the awful suspicion he's not as serious as Leigh, and she's head over heels in love with him.'

Ralph frowned heavily. 'You don't think he loves her?'

'Oh, I'm sure he does, in his own way. It's more than that. Something Leigh said to me earlier made me anxious. Though she tried to hide it, I could see she was upset when she told me there were definitely to be no children. Morgan didn't want to be tied down by them,' Una enlarged carefully. 'That doesn't sound to me like the action of a man ready to settle down.'

Her husband's face took on a harness more often seen on his son. 'You're right, it doesn't.'

Una sighed. 'What are we going to do, Ralph?'

Ralph was still frowning. 'I'm not quite sure. If you're right—and I must admit my own suspicions have troubled me—something must be done.' He looked across at his wife. 'Una, for once I'm glad you told me your doubts.'

Una smiled apologetically. 'I didn't want to burden you, darling, but with my only child's happiness at stake...'

Ralph nodded. 'I understand. Unfortunately this couldn't have happened at a worse time. Una, my dear, there's something I have to tell you, in strictest confidence.'

'Of course you can trust me, darling. What is it?'

Ralph rose. 'We'll go to the library. Frankly, I could do with a brandy.'

As she left the room on his arm, Una's curiosity warred with a huge, satisfied, catlike grin.

In the study, totally unaware of what was going on in her absence, Leigh watched as Morgan opened the safe and rifled through the contents until he found what he wanted. He turned with a small, faded velvet box in his hand and flipped open the lid with his thumb. Leigh couldn't smother a gasp as the exquisite ring was revealed.

'Well, what do you think of it, now that you've seen it?'

'It's beautiful,' she was compelled to answer honestly.

'Better than a curtain ring, isn't it?' he jeered softly.

She should have guessed that he would find an opportunity to mock her words. 'No, not unless it was given with genuine feeling.'

Morgan's gaze narrowed speculatively, then he removed the ring from its box and captured her left hand. 'So, if I put the ring on your finger like this,' it slipped on as if it had been made for her, 'and said, wear it, darling, as a token of my love, you'd be satisfied?' he probed cynically.

Deep inside her, something tore wide open with a scream of pain. She raised eyes to his that were dark with hurt and glittering with unshed tears. 'Ridicule me all you like, but you know as well as I do that mere words aren't enough. They have to come from the heart.'

Morgan merely looked amused. 'Perhaps I don't have one. Or perhaps, not one that could ever respond to the kind of woman you are. So make do with what you have, Leigh. My mother's ring, a big society wedding—and my name for as long as the marriage lasts. Afterwards I promise you a divorce settlement that won't be sniffed at.'

Leigh tugged her hand free and turned her back on him, feeling chilled. 'That's big of you, but I don't want your money.'

'I shouldn't be too hasty in cutting off your nose to spite your face. You'd be free to go anywhere in the world you liked. You might even catch yourself a millionaire. Think of it, Leigh. The perfect cure for a broken heart.'

Hurt and anger warred inside her until she rounded on him like a cornered animal, eyes wide, chest heaving. 'Listen to me, you...you... I don't want your rotten money! I don't want to travel the world, and I don't want a millionaire! When this marriage is over, that's it. I won't ever marry again. You can call me a fool, and laugh in my face, but I've known for some time that if I can't have you, I don't want anybody. I love you, and I won't be made to feel ashamed of it.'

'Bravo! A magnificent performance, almost on a par with your mother,' Morgan applauded. 'And in between your bouts of grand passion, no doubt you too will be finding a little light relief where you can.'

She was stunned; her head went back as if he had actually struck her. The pain of it was in her eyes as she tried to turn away. She struggled as Morgan caught her, finding her hands and trapping them behind her back in one vice-like hand. The other hand he used to tilt her face up to his. Although she tried to evade the manoeuvre, eventually he won. Swallowing madly, she kept her lids lowered, refusing to look at him.

Morgan wasn't having that. 'Look at me,' he commanded abruptly. When she still refused, he lowered his head and pressed a short punishing kiss on her lips. When he raised his head again, she stared at him from stormy green eyes.

It was a moment before he spoke, and when he did a nerve ticked away in his jaw. 'Dammit, Leigh, why not give it up now, before it's too late?'

'Let me go.'

'Not until you promise to end this ridiculous game you're playing,' he refused tensely.

Leigh closed her eyes briefly. 'It's not a game, and I won't make a promise I know I can't keep.'

'God! Don't you have any pride at all? I tell you I don't love you and you know I never will, yet still you come back for more. It's crazy!' he exploded irritably, eyes boring into hers as if to find an acceptable answer there.

'Obviously not,' she choked. They were pressed so closely together, she could feel his heart thudding as strongly as her own. Awareness was a *frisson* of excitement that swiftly spread to every tingling nerve. She realised then that she still had some pride, because she didn't want him to know just how much his nearness affected her. 'Morgan, please, let me go now,' she said again, breathily.

It was the wrong thing to say, for at once the quality of his gaze changed, turning from irritation to an awareness of the scent and feel of her in his arms. The very air about them seemed to shimmer then go still as they communicated without words. The hand that cupped her face became a caress, and Morgan gave a groan way down in his throat.

She saw his intent and her lids dropped. Her 'No!' died under the first sensual assault of his lips, and with it went the will to fight. She surrendered with a whimper of need that drew an answering moan from Morgan. It was like lighting a fuse. All the aching longing tumbled out in a furious flurry of kisses that drained the breath from their lungs and left them gasping. Miraculously, her hands were free, and she entwined them around him, pressing herself close even as his arms sought to draw her closer.

It was a dizzying madness, and Leigh never felt him carry her to the nearest chair and sit down, cradling her across his lap. She was lost in a realm of delicious sensations as his hand caressed the length of her spine, down over her thigh and up again to enclose her breast, creating even more havoc as his fingers teased the proudly jutting peak.

Her head fell back as his fingers pushed aside the strap of her dress until her breast lay bare. His lips trailed a scorching path down her neck, lingering on the frantically beating pulse at its base before finally reaching their goal.

The pleasure wrought by his tongue and lips made her arch her body in to him, wanting the delicious havoc never to end. Her hands moved restlessly through his hair and over his shoulders, longing for the freedom to touch him as he was touching her. She cried out softly, and at once his mouth lifted to cover hers once more and draw her into an erotic whirlpool that made her long for the ultimate satisfaction.

Where it would all have ended she neither knew, nor, in that moment, cared. But Morgan hadn't travelled so swiftly or so far along the road as she. With a tormented groan he tore his mouth from hers, to stare down into her love-drugged face, chest heaving and with eyes in which the flames of desire still burned with a vengeance.

'Dear God, why can't I keep my hands off you? Why must it be you of all women who tempts me almost beyond endurance?' he muttered hoarsely. 'I've known other, more beautiful women, and yet it's you—you who fills me with this driving need to possess.'

He sounded so confused that her eyes softened and she cupped her hand to his cheek. The answer was so absurdly simple. It was a wonder neither of them had seen it before. She should have, because only he could stir her to the same depths. 'Oh, Morgan, you know why,' she told him softly.

Morgan froze at the expression in her eyes, his own narrowing as he read what she meant there. 'No!'

'Yes,' she insisted quickly. 'You love me. Why don't you stop fighting it, as I have? What we feel is love—there can be no other answer.'

'No!' he cut her off sharply, rejection in every inch of him. 'No, I won't accept that. It's just sex, Leigh. My body wants you, that's all. And though I may crave to lose myself in you, it will never happen. Because women like you, once you've got your claws in, won't let go. I've seen it with my father, and it won't happen to me. So get rid of the notion that I was fated to love you. It's lust, pure and simple. Christ, I could never love *you*.'

That last was said with such a wealth of revulsion in his voice that Leigh felt sick. Each word had sent an icy spear into her heart. But she could only take so much pain before the need to strike back sparked into life.

'Couldn't you?' she scorned. 'I think you already do, Morgan. Haven't you ever heard of protesting too much? I think it's already too late!' she went on, her voice gaining strength as she struggled to her feet and rearranged her dress.

Morgan was on his feet too, hands lifting to smooth down the hair her fingers had raked through mere minutes ago. 'It's never too late to cut out the rotten piece of the apple. And that's what I'd do, Leigh, if ever I were foolish enough to really find myself loving you. I'm afraid you've miscalculated. It hasn't happened yet, and I'm going to make certain it doesn't in the future.'

Leigh shivered at the coldness of his look, but she raised her chin defiantly because she knew she had uncovered the truth. Morgan *did* love her, however vehement the denial. It was so obvious it was blinding. It had crept upon them unawares, but he was refusing to accept it. 'It's dangerous to be too proud. You can't fight love, it's too strong. Killing it might not be as easy as you think.'

He laughed, once more completely in control. 'You talk as if some ancient and vengeful god will strike me down for blasphemy! Don't worry about me. If I say I can do it, then you'd better believe that I can, and will.'

Leigh held his forceful gaze, feeling the strength of his will-power trying to crush her new-found belief. 'I don't believe you.'

His nostrils flared, the only sign of his anger. 'Then, sweetheart, I suggest you watch this space,' he declared cuttingly.

A chill ran up her spine as she held his gaze a moment longer. She had been convinced by the revelation, when it first struck her, that they were caught in something stronger than both of them, but now her confidence wavered. Was he stronger than this feeling they shared? Only time would tell.

Knowing Morgan as she did, to try and convince him not to fight it would only be fuelling his determination. All she could do was watch and wait.

'We'd better go back,' she said as evenly as she could. 'They'll be wondering what's happened to us.'

'No, they won't,' Morgan responded drily as he opened the door. 'They'll know exactly what's been taking us so long. After all, darling, we're madly in love, aren't we?'

Unseen by him, her eyes closed. She had just given him a rod to beat her with, and he was angry enough to use it.

CHAPTER SEVEN

'DARLING, you look enchanting,' Una declared as she gave a final twitch to the layers of white satin and lace wedding dress, and smoothed the yards of exquisite veiling, held in place by a glittering tiara.

Leigh's eyes flickered to their twin reflections in the cheval-glass. They could have been sisters instead of mother and daughter. The thought did nothing to cheer her.

'I've always said you pay for dressing. That, at least, you get from me,' Una added in satisfaction. Smoothing down her own cream silk suit, she caught sight of her own reflection. Her attention was instantly diverted, and she reached into her purse for her lipstick.

Leigh watched the primping with growing irritation. Ever since she had woken up, people had been fussing around her until now she felt stifled. 'Mother, would you mind? I'd like a few minutes to myself.'

Una gave her reflection one final inspection, then turned to her daughter with a smile. 'Very well, darling. Ten minutes. I'll bring something medicinal back with me. You need something to put some colour into your cheeks. Goodness knows, you look as if you're going to your own execution, not your wedding. Do for heaven's sake try to smile, darling.' The parting order was punctuated by the closing of the bedroom door.

Thankfully alone, for a short time at least, Leigh stared down at the emerald that glinted on her right hand. The night Morgan had placed it on her finger he had mockingly declared that they were madly in love. Over the last four weeks they had certainly given a good impression of it at every opportunity. She doubted that anyone would guess that only one of them truly loved.

112

Or, should she say, only one admitted to it? Whatever, in less than an hour from now Morgan would be slipping a golden wedding-band on to her finger, compounding the lie.

She shivered. Before everyone they had lied; she alone knew the reality of his coldness, his remoteness. He hadn't attempted to touch her since that evening, except in public, and there were times when he had seemed to look right through her. He had told her what he would do, that he would kill any feeling he might have, and his determination was chilling.

She had been helpless to do anything other than stand and watch him reject her claim that her love was in fact mutual. He had done nothing to make her own feelings wither, but had distanced himself, alienating her to a spot where she was the hapless observer of his clinical brain at work. It had been unnerving to find herself with an ardent lover one moment, saying and doing things it was all too easy to believe in, and then be cast adrift by a rapid return to that chilling remoteness.

Such behaviour had made her glad to have her time filled with trips to London to have her wedding-dress fitted, and to purchase a complete trousseau. Not that she had shown a great deal of interest in the clothes. In fact, she could scarcely remember what lay packed into the new suite of luggage stacked in the corner of her bedroom.

Luggage that would soon be winging its way to the Caribbean. Ralph had been as good as his word. He had made an unscheduled trip to town, and when he returned he had laid before them the details of the honeymoon he had arranged. Three weeks on one of the Caribbean's small, exotic islands.

It should have been a taste of paradise, but Leigh knew it was going to be something quite different.

A tap on the door brought her head up, and in the mirror she watched as her mother re-entered the room, carrying a glass.

Una picked her way across to the bed and handed her a half-glass of sherry. 'Here, drink this, and for heaven's sake don't spill any. I've got five minutes, then I must go with the bridesmaids. Morgan left fifteen minutes ago, and Ralph's waiting for you downstairs.' She stood back to look her daughter over critically. 'Darling, I wish you'd smile a little.'

Leigh drained the glass and felt some warmth return to her insides. She set the glass aside and produced the smile her mother wanted. 'Weren't you ever nervous, Mother?' The easiest way to divert Una was to turn the conversation her way.

'Me, nervous? When I was on the verge of getting what I wanted? Never, darling. And you won't be nervous either, if you just remember you're getting the man you want.' She eyed her daughter slyly. 'Morgan is who you want, isn't he?'

At least in that she didn't have to lie. 'You know he is.'

Una patted her cheek. 'Then cheer up, darling. Now, I really must go.' She aimed one of those kisses at Leigh's cheek that was never designed to make contact, and made for the door, disappearing through it with a wave of her hand.

Leigh stood and surveyed herself solemnly in the cheval-glass. Down below she heard car doors shutting and the sound of engines disappearing. Soon it would be her turn. Morgan was already waiting in the church. She wondered if he would find her beautiful, but knew that, even if he did, he probably wouldn't show it.

'Time to go, Leigh.'

She jumped at the soft sound of Ralph's voice, not having heard his knock, and swung around. He looked a little uncomfortable in his morning suit, yet was endearingly the same man who had given her love and comfort all these years. It made her want to throw herself into his arms and cry out all her despair, but she wasn't a little girl any more, and he couldn't help her with this pain.

So instead she gave him her first real smile of the day. 'You look very distinguished,' she said fondly, and, collecting her bouquet from the chair it lay on, walked over to him.

Ralph cleared his throat noisily. 'And you look enchanting. I couldn't be more proud of you, my dear. I know Morgan will be too.' He held out his arms and she went into them.

'I hope you're right. I love him so very much. I only want to make him happy,' she whispered against his weathered cheek. In her heart she knew that hope, the eternal phoenix, expected much of today. The ceremony they were to go through meant a great deal to her and she couldn't believe that it wouldn't mean something to Morgan. In God's house she wouldn't lie. Every vow would be sacred. Only the truth had a place there, and when she saw him waiting for her she would know it, because he wouldn't be able to hide it.

Ralph patted her shoulder gently. 'You will, my dear, you will. And I intend to make sure he makes you happy, too,' he added on a grim note.

Leigh eased away to look at him in surprise. 'Ralph?'

'Oh, take no notice of an old man. All I meant was that I don't hand you over to him lightly. I've cared for you for a long time, and I can't seem to get out of the habit,' he dismissed with a laugh, and glanced at his watch. 'Right now, Morgan will be as nervous as any man can be. Let's go and put him out of his misery.' He held out his arm and she took it, returning his smile even as she wondered who was going to put her out of *her* misery.

It was only a short ride to the church, and in no time at all they were inside. This was her last chance, she knew, to change her mind and refuse to go through with it. Then the organist struck up the bridal march, and all her doubts vanished.

Moving slowly forward on Ralph's arm, she knew she would marry Morgan in any circumstances. Perhaps there was more of her mother in her than she thought, for, rightly or wrongly, she wanted to be his wife, wanted him to be hers. Who was to say she might not find happiness? It was an acceptable risk. She doubted she would find it without him.

Through her veil her eyes were fixed on Morgan's tall, proud figure as he waited for her. Her heart swelled. He looked magnificent in the morning suit, so very handsome. She longed for him to turn and look at her. How could he doubt her love if he saw her? How could he deny his own feelings?

She was almost upon him when he did finally turn, as if compelled. Through the veil her eyes searched his face eagerly. What she saw made her heart freeze and she missed a step. She felt Ralph look down at her sharply and forced her icy lips into a smile. She walked on in a haze of pain. There had been nothing there. His eyes had been as remote as the moon—without any light or warmth. She stopped beside him, knowing he had done what he said he would. Whatever he had felt he had killed. There hadn't even been desire. Only a vast, cold void.

The service began, and she took part like an automaton going through the motions. The hand she placed in his for him to put his ring on her finger was icy and trembling, and she wanted to cry out in pain. He had beaten her. That look had told her all, and destroyed her hopes at a blow. What was she going to do? She couldn't let him see his victory. *Must* not let him see. From the wreckage she dredged up her pride.

When Morgan lifted her veil to kiss her, she knew she looked pale, but hoped he would put that down to bridal nerves. His lips were cool, the kiss thankfully brief. She couldn't have borne more. Then they were walking back down the aisle and out into the sunlight. It was over; she was his wife. The wife he felt absolutely nothing for— while she loved him beyond everything. Oh, God, she couldn't break down! There were photographs to take. She smiled until she felt her face were about to break, amazed that nobody seemed to realise there was anything wrong.

In a hail of confetti, rice and laughter, at last they climbed into the limousine that was waiting to take them back to the house. Beside her, Morgan relaxed back against the seat with a heartfelt sigh.

'Thank God that's over.'

Leigh steeled herself to glance sideways at him. Nothing was wrong. She had to make him believe that. She saw the bright pieces of confetti stuck in his hair and winced. Do something, her brain urged. Don't let him guess. She reached out a hand to pick them off, and found her wrist caught in the vice of his hand. Blue eyes raked her in sharp suspicion.

She swallowed, but smiled, knowing her task was going to be very hard—next to impossible—but vital now. She had to put up a front. 'It's only confetti,' she explained, and opened her palm to show him the crushed pieces.

Firmly he set her hand down on her lap. 'Thanks, but I'll brush it out later.'

'Afraid my touch will contaminate you, Morgan?' She laughed bitterly, and cursed herself for a fool as his eyes narrowed.

'What game are you playing now?' he barked harshly. 'Whatever it is, forget it.'

Game? This wasn't a game, it was survival! 'Why?' she challenged huskily. 'I've got nothing to lose.' No truer word had been spoken!

'And nothing to gain either,' he countered smoothly. 'I was wondering how long it would take. Barely half an hour and you think you own me! That ring changes nothing.'

She glanced down at it, knowing the truth of what he said. 'It makes me your wife,' she argued.

'But gives you none of the privileges, so back off, Leigh, before you get hurt,' he advised coldly.

More than she already was? What a joke! She had gambled for high stakes, but she hadn't really been prepared to lose. She had hoped...but that had been so childish. So naïve. 'And if I don't?' Green eyes lifted to hold his, and he drew in a frustrated breath before shrugging and looking away.

'It's your funeral. If you choose to ignore my warnings and the rules, then I won't feel obliged to stick to them either,' he said bluntly.

Leigh moved the emerald to join her wedding-band, making an organised retreat because she refused to be routed. 'Rules were made to be broken,' she reminded him. She had broken so many herself, and now she had nothing—except her pride.

Her answer brought his head round, expression remote. 'Then you do so at your own risk.'

Risk. She had thought this marriage an acceptable one only a short while ago. So full of rosy dreams, it was pitiful. Yet she still tried to salvage something. She twisted in her seat, her hand clutching his arm. 'Why must we fight? Can't we try——?' She wasn't allowed to finish.

Morgan removed her hand and dropped it. 'No,' he stated firmly. 'But don't lose heart. Your first attempt to get round me might have failed, but I'm sure you have others up your sleeve. Una would have trained you well.'

Her teeth came together in a little snap. 'And what does that mean?'

Morgan grinned. 'I'm referring to Una's patented, tried and true method: how to get your man in ten easy lessons. Lesson one: first trap him. Number two: put a ring through his nose.' He held up her hand on which his rings glittered. 'Three: make him happy in his prison. Ring any bells, does it?'

Leigh stared at him, the lead weight growing in her stomach. Yes, she knew what he meant. She had seen Una use those very methods countless times. 'That's just coincidence. I didn't plan any of it,' she denied unevenly.

'So you don't plan to make me enjoy our marriage so much I won't want to break it off when the time comes?' he queried cynically.

She sat back, head averted. Yes, she had wanted to do that, though it wasn't a plan. It was because she loved him, knew that, if only he let her, she could make him happy.

'I'm sorry if I've upset your plans.' Morgan's voice was heavy with amusement.

Leigh glanced round. Catching his eyes, she remembered what she had seen there, and her determination not to let him see he had beaten her so easily grew. She smiled and shook her head. 'You haven't,' she denied lightly.

At once his face was wiped clean of laughter. 'Only a fool would carry on with a plan when all the details are known,' he said discouragingly.

It felt good to fight him. It stopped the terrible pain getting through. 'You're right, but you're forgetting one thing. I don't happen to have a plan,' Leigh retorted mockingly. No, no plan. This was basic survival. Take each day as it came. It would get easier. It had to!

Morgan patently didn't believe her, but was forestalled from saying so by their arrival back at the house. In the following hours they had no time to themselves, for which she was heartily grateful. There were speeches and toasts, the cake to cut, and an endless circulation among the guests. Through it all, Leigh was ever conscious of Morgan's arm at her waist, publicly claiming what he privately couldn't wait to be rid of.

By the time she went up to change for their trip to the airport, Leigh had had quite enough of her own wedding. The party was due to carry on well into the early hours, but she would be glad to get away from the strain of pretending everything was all right.

What she needed, she decided wryly as she hung the lovely dress on its hanger and slipped on the blue silk suit Una had decreed was just right for travelling, was a good holiday. Somehow, she didn't think their honeymoon was going to fall into that category. It wasn't funny, and she beat back hot tears. There was no time for that now. Later, there would be all the time in the world.

When she descended the stairs again, Morgan was already waiting, having changed into a lightweight blue suit, Una and Ralph at his side. Her mother came across and gave her a brief brush of the lips on her cheek.

'He's all yours now, darling. Good luck.'

'Thank you, Mother,' Leigh responded drily, and turned to Ralph who held out his arms to her. Suddenly choked, she held him tight.

'Be happy, my dear,' he said softly as he released her and faced his son. 'Be sure and look after her, Morgan.'

'Oh, I will, Dad.' There was mockery in his eyes as he held out his hand to Leigh. 'Come along, Mrs Fairfax, or we'll miss our flight,' he added drily.

Leigh took his hand, aware of the icy fingers tightening about her heart at the sound of her new name. They left amid a flurry of ribald jokes and shouted best wishes. Once clear of the drive, Morgan stopped to remove the strings of tin cans that had been tied to the bumper. The rest of the journey to the airport passed in silence. There was something forbidding about Morgan's profile as he concentrated on his driving that inhibited speech. Leigh had nothing to say anyway. The three weeks stretched ahead of her like a prison sentence. They would be thrown together constantly, and somehow she had to survive it. The trouble was, she didn't know how. She had only ever had one plan, and that had been to love him. But that had been made with hope. Now she knew there was none, she felt lost. Hope had been her sheet-anchor, but now she was at the mercy of Morgan's stormy seas.

It was already dark when they made their last transfer from light aircraft to the waiting car at the island's small airport. Leigh was bone-weary, glad to sit back and close her eyes for what the friendly driver had informed them was only a short ride.

She had slept a little on the plane, then watched the in-flight movie and read some magazines, all the while very much aware of Morgan's uncommunicative figure beside her. He had engrossed himself in a paperback novel, effectively shutting her out. She had tried talking to him, but his answers had been so short that she had given up in the end and picked up her own book. But her thoughts had been miles away, just as they were now.

Tonight was their wedding-night. She shivered at the thought. How could she share a bed with him, knowing the coldness that would stretch between them? Yet what could she do? Nothing, save keep up the façade. Pretend she hadn't seen what she had in his eyes. Go on as if she still had confidence. Ride the punches and come out fighting. She absolutely would not give in to self-pity.

The bungalow was isolated, though there were others discreetly dotted along the bay, their porter informed them. Privacy was ensured here if you wanted it. For those who didn't there was the hotel itself. In the playground of the rich, this complex catered only for the élite.

Leigh was too tired and discouraged to be impressed. When the cheerful islander left, she felt the isolation close in about her, locking her in with Morgan. She shivered again.

'Damn.'

She heard Morgan's muffled curse from the bedroom and forced tired legs to take her to the door. 'What's the matter?'

Morgan looked at her, face set. 'The bed,' he said shortly.

Her eyebrows rose. Whether from tiredness or misery, or both, she laughed. 'Isn't that supposed to be my line? In all the best romances——'

'Look at it, damn it,' he cut her off.

She looked, and her heart sank, all desire to laugh fading. There was one bed, and it was king-size. It was also very definitely designed for lovers. From satin-padded heart-shaped headboard, to silk sheets.

Leigh bit her lip. 'Ralph must have asked for the honeymoon suite.'

Morgan took a deep breath. 'My God, if he weren't my father...'

She swallowed a giant lump in her throat. 'He thought he was giving us a surprise.' Oh, God, she didn't want to stay here!

'He's damn well succeeded. But don't let this give you any ideas, Leigh. We may have to share this...creation, but it's big enough so that we don't have to touch. Pick which side you want, and make sure you stay there.'

She paled, angry at his arrogant assumption that she would want to do anything else. 'What are you afraid of, Morgan? That I'll lose control—or that you will?' she snapped back defensively, and then almost laughed at the idea. 'Well, don't worry, all I intend to do when I get into bed is sleep,' she added caustically, and hoped desperately that she would be able to do so, and block out this whole miserable day.

Deciding to unpack in the morning, she took only night things from her case and carried them through to the bathroom. She showered quickly, dried herself on a bathsheet then slipped into the lacy piece of nothing Una had packed for her to wear tonight. She caught sight of herself in the mirror and flushed. It was so revealing, so obviously seductive, she didn't think she'd be able to walk back into the bedroom in it. If there was a négligé to match she didn't know where it was. Short of wrapping herself in a towel, though, she had no option.

The long side slits parted at every step, revealing her long shapely legs as she returned to the bedroom. Morgan was there, stripped down to his trousers, chest and feet bare. She stopped dead, flushing as he ran his eyes over her.

'Planning on a spot of seduction, were you?' he drawled in amusement. 'It almost seems a pity to let it go to waste.' She held her breath as he came towards her, eyes widening as he reached out to brush a finger over her lips, making her gasp. 'Almost,' he said softly, and walked past her and into the bathroom, closing the door with a firmness that shut her out of his life.

Leigh swallowed back painful tears as she sank into bed, burying her face in the pillows. Fool! Even now she hoped, not willing to accept it. Well, she had to.

It was a long time after Morgan joined her in the big bed that she was finally able to sleep.

CHAPTER EIGHT

LEIGH awoke to a comfortable feeling of warmth and security. Her startled senses soon discovered why. Some time during the night, both she and Morgan had gravitated to the centre of the bed, and now she lay held against him, his arm around her waist, his body fitted along the length of her like a glove.

It could have been her own startled movement that woke him, for suddenly Morgan sighed, his legs moving, before stopping abruptly when they came into contact with hers. She knew that he had realised instantly, just as she had, what had happened. She turned her head to look at him and saw the shock in his eyes.

'Hi,' she greeted gruffly, mouth dry as tinder.

Morgan didn't answer; he didn't need to. She saw shock change to anger and then contempt, and abruptly he was moving away from her, flinging himself from the bed, careless of his nakedness. She watched miserably as he dug a pair of swimming-trunks from his case, tugged them on, gathered up a towel and left the room without once looking at her.

Leigh rolled on to her back, arm flung over her eyes. She needed no words to tell her that her discovery of yesterday was not a dream. He felt nothing for her but contempt. Her body seemed to ache all over with the stress of it as she sat up and climbed wearily from the bed.

She padded to the window and thrust open the shutters. The view that met her eyes was breathtaking. The veranda was hung about with all manner of exotic blooms that dazzled the eyes and gave off a heady perfume. Beyond that, through the palms, she could see the brilliant white sand and intense blue of the sea and sky.

In the midst of all that beauty she saw Morgan's stiff-backed figure as he strode down into the water and dived in. The anger in every flashing stroke of his arms made her bite her lip. She would have loved to have gone for a swim herself, but not now. The wound was still too new.

Instead, she showered and changed into shorts and T-shirt, and unpacked their cases. When that was done she went through to the lounge. Beside the telephone was a typed list of services, and she ordered breakfast for two. Although she had no idea when Morgan would be back, she decided that the best way to go on was to act naturally.

He returned just as the waiter left after arranging their breakfast on the table on the veranda. Leigh watched him approach and sighed inwardly at his closed expression.

'I ordered breakfast,' she stated unnecessarily as he mounted the steps, for he must already have seen the table. His eyes missed nothing, which was why she had felt the need to say something.

'I'll be with you in a moment,' he told her shortly as he passed on into the bungalow.

Leigh pulled a face and sat down, reaching for a hot croissant and spreading it with jam, though she had scant appetite. Morgan joined her within a few minutes and tucked into the meal. Clearly nothing had upset his appetite, she thought waspishly, then sighed. Feeling bitter wasn't going to help. There had to be a way to get through the next three weeks without having her emotions torn to shreds.

'How was the water?' she asked as the silence lengthened.

'Warm. You should try it.'

'Perhaps I will, later,' she said, and waited for him to say more, but he didn't, and it stretched her nerves unbearably. When he sat back, sipping at a second cup of coffee, she tried again. 'What are we going to do today?'

Morgan drained the cup before looking at her. 'I don't know about you, but I've got work to do.'

She knew her jaw dropped but couldn't help it. 'You brought *work* with you?'

'A new project. I thought it would be a good time to get started on it.' His eyes were a definite challenge.

Her heart thudded and she felt sick with humiliation. 'And what am I supposed to do?' she demanded thickly.

'That's entirely up to you.'

Blinding anger came to her rescue. 'That's very kind of you. I have *carte blanche* then, to do as I like?'

His eyes narrowed. 'Within reason.'

'And what exactly do you class as reasonable, Morgan?' Her throat was so tight the words hurt as they emerged.

'I don't expect my wife to be seen with other men.'

It would have been simple to remind him that he was the only man she wanted, but she refused to keep leading with her chin.

'Or with you, either,' she responded acidly. 'At least I know where I stand. I'll try to keep what you said in mind, but don't be surprised if I ignore it.' She pushed herself to her feet. 'I might as well be off, then. I'll see you later.'

Anger took her down the steps and along the path to the hotel, but, once out of sight, her shoulders slumped. He was rubbing it in, underlining the point, and she hated him for it. A sigh escaped her. No, she didn't hate him. She wished she could, but it seemed impossible. Well, she knew one thing, she wasn't going to let him get away with it. She'd be damned if she let him see that she cared one way or the other that he was deliberately shutting her out.

There were plenty of people around the hotel, mostly sunbathing, but some were down at a small jetty and she made her way there without any real thought of joining in. However, as soon as she saw the windsurfers, her interest was piqued. She had always wanted to learn, and it didn't take very long for Nick, the young instructor, to persuade her to join in the fun.

She thought of going back to the bungalow for lunch, but what was there really to go back to? She decided to stay where she was. If Morgan wanted her, he could come and find her. Consequently, it was late afternoon before she made her way back to the bungalow, tired but happy. Morgan was on the veranda when she came up from the beach. She sensed his anger even before she saw the set lines of his face.

'Where have you been?' he demanded as soon as she came level with him.

Leigh raised her eyebrows at him. My God, he had a nerve! 'How did the work go?' she asked, ignoring his question.

He caught her arm. 'Damn it, didn't you hear what I said?'

She held his gaze. 'Yes, I heard, but I don't believe I have to answer. You said we were to do what we liked, you didn't want to know, so I won't bore you with details. Excuse me, I have to shower and change.'

He let her go because he had no option, but he was furious. In fact, he was still angry when they went to dinner, and it made Leigh fume. Having chosen to ignore her, he had no right to be angry when she went her own way. He had made his choice. He couldn't have it both ways.

They were eating their dinner in the sort of atmosphere that didn't help digestion when a figure came to a halt beside their table. Leigh looked up. Recognising Nick, the young instructor, she smiled warmly.

'Hi, how are you feeling? Any aches and pains?' Nick asked, grinning confidentially.

Leigh laughed, aware that Morgan had stopped eating and was listening. 'Not many. I really enjoyed myself,' she added, just to goad him.

'Good. Then perhaps we can get together again tomorrow?' Nick went on, completely unawares.

'I'd like that.' Though she didn't look at him, she could feel Morgan tensing.

'Great. I'll look forward to seeing you then.' Nick smiled at her, nodded to Morgan and went on his way.

With his departure, Leigh was very much aware that the barometer had dropped and storm warnings were out. She glanced at Morgan's grim face then concentrated on her food. Talk about a double standard! He was like the salesman who told his customers, you can have any colour you want, so long as it's black!

'Who was that?'

She looked up, shrugging. 'Just someone I met today,' she said airily, and rather enjoyed seeing Morgan's chest heave as he took a deep breath.

'So I gather,' he gritted through his teeth. 'Are you seeing him tomorrow?'

Leigh rested her chin on her hand and looked squarely at him, 'I thought I might.'

'I see,' he said grimly, and Leigh wondered just what it was he did see as he returned his attention to his food.

He scarcely said another word to her for the rest of the meal, and when they returned to the bungalow he took up the files he had been working on and settled down with a glass of whisky at his elbow. Leigh fumed inwardly at his behaviour and took herself off to bed, reading a book until she felt tired enough to sleep.

She had no idea what time Morgan joined her; all she did know was that when she awoke next morning they were together in the middle of the big bed once more. Almost at the same time, Morgan woke, and he rolled away from her again with a muffled curse. She turned over to see him pull on bathing-trunks and gather up his towel. This time he threw her a tight look as he went out. Leigh lay back with a sigh, limbs trembling. How could he blame her for what their bodies did unconsciously? But it seemed he did. The unfairness was another blow to her morale, but it also kept her anger bubbling away. For which she was thankful, because she needed it to hide her vulnerability.

She was eating breakfast when he came back and stopped beside the table.

'Are you going to see that man today?' he demanded curtly.

If she didn't know better, she would have imagined he was jealous. But she did know. 'Yes, I am,' she retorted. 'You can work, I intend to have some fun.'

His hands tightened on the towel draped about his neck. 'With him?'

'Why not?' My God, he had a nerve!

'The man's a shark. I've seen his sort before. They prey on rich, bored wives!' Morgan declared angrily.

Leigh stared at him incredulously. 'Am I hearing correctly? Are you concerned for *me*? Knowing, as I do, what you think of me, I find it very hard to believe. Shouldn't you be talking to him?' she cried mockingly.

Morgan gritted his teeth. 'Don't be a damn fool. Can't you see he only wants one thing?'

Angry tears warred with hurt ones. How could he? What a hypocrite! Talking as if he cared when she knew damn well he didn't! Her chair scraped back as she stood up. 'Perhaps he does, but it's more than you do! You've made that very plain. Well, if you've decided to shut me out, I can do what I like. And it just so happens that I like sharks!' she finished, and pushed past him to run down the steps, heading into the trees, so angry she could spit.

She dashed her hands over her eyes as she walked. Morgan had no right to be acting like this. She had accepted her defeat without a word of recrimination. So she certainly didn't deserve this. He didn't care, so why pretend he did? It was only sour grapes. He didn't want her but he wouldn't let anyone else have her either. He probably thought she was showing him up. A wife on her honeymoon didn't spend her time with another man. Certainly not his wife, whether he wanted her or not!

Her footsteps slowed. He didn't want her in any sense of the word. Whereas she... But it was pointless thinking that way. Best not to think of it at all, because it hurt so much. If she thought too much, she'd fall apart. An hour might seem like eternity, but it wasn't. Fill up each hour and the day was gone, that was her plan. So that she'd be too tired for anything but sleep when she climbed into that huge mocking bed. But that was taking her back to dangerous ground, and she shook her head, shaking off the mood before it grew too black.

She had calmed down by the time she reached the jetty, and threw herself into enjoying herself with a vengeance. But she had only been there half an hour when she surfaced from another ducking to find Morgan watching her from the beach. Her heart jolted. Why had he come? To spy? She would have ignored him, but Nick had seen him too and had already started to drag the board shorewards. Leigh had to follow.

'Hi,' she heard Nick say as she waded out to join them. 'Were you thinking of taking lessons too? Your wife's pretty good already.'

Morgan's face turned to stone, his body filled with a peculiar tension. His gaze flickered to Leigh then away again. 'Thanks, but I can already windsurf. If you don't mind, I want a few words with my wife.'

'Sure,' Nick grinned, 'no sweat. You can hire a board any time you want to,' he added, waved a hand to Leigh and went to join the other learners.

They stood staring at each other, Leigh defensively, Morgan with an odd look in his eye.

'So,' he said at last, 'he's the sports instructor.'

She crossed her arms, eyes flashing. '*I* never said he was anything else,' she pointed out.

'You could have put me straight.'

'I could, but you were having too much fun jumping to conclusions. It's a habit you have with me. First Gerald Villiers, then Toby and now Nick.'

Morgan stared at her for a long moment, then out to sea, running a hand around his neck. 'All the same, I don't want you coming here any more.'

'Maybe not, but I'll go where I please. You meet an interesting class of person here. If you added it up, the wealth on paper of the men here would be millions. I have every intention of checking each one out!' she taunted with bravado.

Morgan turned back to her, a grim smile about his lips. 'You're a scrappy fighter, Leigh. You always were. As a kid you never hesitated to go into the attack—on the principle that it was the best defence. You've got better at it. I used to be able to read your moves as if you'd telegraphed them, but I didn't see this coming. I take it this is my punishment for ignoring you?'

She laughed. How could he get everything so wrong? 'Think what you like, I don't care any more. Now, if you don't mind, I have a lesson to finish.'

His hand shot out to prevent her leaving. 'If you want to learn to windsurf, I'll teach you.'

Leigh stared at him, suspecting her hearing. 'What?' she asked with a disbelieving laugh.

A nerve ticked in his jaw. 'I said I'd teach you,' he repeated grittily.

'I wouldn't put you to such trouble. Think about your work.'

Anger flared in his eyes. 'That can wait. Do you want to learn or not?' he demanded.

'That depends on the reason you want to teach me,' Leigh countered. 'If it's for the reason I think it is, then I'll go on the way I am, thank you.'

For a moment he looked astounded, as if he hadn't really expected her to refuse. Then he drew a deep breath. 'If that's the way you want it.'

If he had only shown some sign that he wanted to teach her, wanted her company, she would have jumped at the chance. But his offer was simply a means of keeping a watchful eye on her, and that she wouldn't stand for.

'It is,' she replied staunchly.

Morgan made no answer, he simply turned and walked away. Leigh watched him go with a sense of defeat, not victory. It felt as if she was cutting off her nose to spite her face, but she couldn't risk the hurt of knowing he

tolerated her presence because he mistrusted her. Biting
her lip, she turned her back on him, making her way
down to where the figures in the water wavered mistily.

That night she found it impossible to sleep. For a while
she lay there listening to Morgan's steady breathing. He
was so close, she only had to reach out to touch him,
but he might as well have been on the moon. She had
returned to the bungalow at lunchtime to be greeted by
a studied politeness that was chilling. She had managed
to hide her dismay behind a politeness of her own,
keeping her words short and to the point. Even so, he
had driven her down to the beach to seek sanctuary from
a situation that was driving knives into her heart.

She hadn't known it could be so lonely, lying next to
someone. She wanted to be held, loved. Unshed tears
clogged her throat and she turned her head on the pillow.
It took every ounce of strength she possessed not to cross
the gap that lay between them and beg him to hold her.

Oh, God, where was her pride? In an agony of self-
disgust, she threw back the covers and climbed out. There
was enough light from the moon to see by and she made
her way out through the lounge on to the veranda. A
cane chair stood nearby and she curled up in it, staring
out into the scent-filled darkness. If two days could bring
her to this, how could she get through the rest? The tears
she had held back fell silently down her cheeks as she
sat there. Gradually, the peace eased her pain, and she
sighed. Going back to that bed was beyond her, though,
and she sat on until a slight sound drew her head round.

Morgan's robed figure stood in the doorway. How long
had he been standing there? What had he seen? She
watched as he moved to the rail and leant against it.

'Did I wake you? I didn't mean to.' Her apology was
automatic.

'I wasn't asleep,' he told her tiredly.

'Oh.' The sound was flat. She couldn't even work up
surprise.

Morgan ran a hand around his neck. 'We can't go on
like this.'

She couldn't agree more. 'What do you suggest?' Returning home was all she had thought of, and that was out of the question.

'That we make the best of a bad situation. We're stuck on this island, whether we like it or not, for the next three weeks. If we want to survive the experience with our sanity intact, I suggest we call a truce.'

'A truce? Do you really think that's possible?' Her tone was sceptical.

'Why not? We never used to have any trouble getting along. We can do it if we try,' he said matter-of-factly.

Leigh closed her eyes and strove to keep her voice level. 'You want us to stop fighting?' Hadn't she suggested that only to be turned down?

'I know you want more,' Morgan returned with an edge, 'but this is the best I can offer. Take it or leave it.'

She looked up then. 'And if I don't?'

'You'd be a fool to reject it,' she was informed shortly, and she knew he was right. She was faced with Hobson's choice. When push came to shove, she'd rather have Morgan as a friend than an enemy, but it was going to be hard.

'Very well, a truce it is. Do we shake on it?' she asked, using flippancy to hide her wounds.

'Let's not push our luck,' Morgan advised, leaving the rail and making for the door. 'Come back to bed, Leigh. Sitting there won't change things.'

It was his night for being right. She knew she had just received the best offer she was going to get, and it wasn't his fault that it wasn't, and never could be, enough. At least this way she would retain some dignity. The very last thing she wanted was his pity.

'You go, I'll follow in a minute.'

'Don't be long. It's getting chilly.'

Ah, but I have my love to keep me warm. The words mocked her even as she nodded and watched him disappear inside. She wished she could find it as easy as him to get into that monstrosity of a bed. It mocked her—a constant reminder of something that never was.

She left it until she was sure Morgan was asleep before finally rejoining him, her heart heavy and with a future that stretched before her like a wilderness.

It was the start of a strange ten days. For all he had said, Morgan was in a volatile mood. His temper would flare up at the oddest times. Yet, for the most part, they had fun. By deliberately forgetting why they were there, Leigh was able to throw herself into everything. Morgan had always been sporty and he taught her to snorkel as well as helping her to perfect her windsurfing technique.

Gradually, she relaxed, allowing her heartache to be lulled by the old friendship they had shared. It helped that there were no more mornings of waking up in his arms. Morgan was always long gone before she stirred. She was aware of his building a wall between them over which it wasn't wise for her to step.

They seemed, on the surface, to be at ease with each other. They explored the island on foot or by Land Rover, shopping in the noisy, colourful markets. Their conversations over lunch were idle, avoiding contentious topics by mutual agreement. They weren't perfect, but they were the happiest days Leigh could remember. She didn't for a moment imagine a miracle was going to happen, but she did come to accept they were building a basis on which their marriage could work—for as long as it lasted.

Only at night, as she lay on her side of the bed, the gap between them as wide as an ocean, did she mourn for what might have been. But she was learning to be practical. If she couldn't have his love, then not to have his contempt would be enough. And if she sometimes longed for him to reach out for her in the night, she kept that strictly to herself.

How long this state of affairs would have gone on, she was never to know, for something happened that changed everything.

* * *

The day had begun hot and grew hotter. They had abandoned their original plan to cross to the other side of the island in favour of staying on the beach. The heat was enervating, leaving them with little energy to do more than laze under the umbrella and swim occasionally to cool off.

'I'm going to get a drink, do you want one?' Morgan asked from where he was lying in the shade on the other side of the pole.

Leigh took her nose from the book she was only half-heartedly reading. 'Please,' she acknowledged, looking up with a smile.

Morgan climbed to his feet. 'I won't be long,' he promised, and strode off towards the bungalow. Leigh's smile faded as she let her eyes follow him.

A small cloud of depression settled about her shoulders. Their truce was working—too well. They were friends again, and the truth was she couldn't stand it. Not that she let him see that, inside, her need was every bit as strong as it had ever been. Which was a good thing, because not even by a look or a touch had he shown any interest in something warmer.

She knew, because she had been watching him constantly, hoping to find a small chink in his sometimes moody armour, but she never had. He was lost to her completely in any meaningful way. What was left was hard to swallow.

Irritably she shut the book and sat up, squinting as the sun glinted off the sea and hurt the eyes. It looked deliciously cool and inviting, just the diversion she needed. She was on her feet in an instant. Jogging down to the water, she quickly waded in until it was deep enough to dive. The water was warm but against her overheated flesh it felt wonderfully cool. She swam for a long time, deliberately blanking her mind of all thought before regretfully wading back out again.

She wrung her hair out as she began walking slowly back up the sand. Shaking her head like a dog, she lifted her arms to smooth it sleekly back—and froze. Morgan had returned. She could see him now, standing under the umbrella watching her. She saw his eyes follow the curves of her golden-limbed body in its minuscule white bikini, and realised just how provocative her stance was. Her first instinct was to drop her arms to her sides— until she saw his eyes again. Even at this distance they scorched her like the sun, and she made a discovery that set her heart racing wildly.

He wanted her. It blazed from him. In that moment the volatile changes of mood of the past two weeks made complete sense. She had thought she knew, but she didn't. It was staggering to realise how wrong she had been, because nothing had changed. The message came to her loud and clear, charged on the sultry air. Dear God, all these weeks he had fooled her! Before the wedding he had shut her out, and would have done so here but for Nick. He *had* been jealous, she was certain of it now. And all those changes of mood were because he was hiding the fact that he did still want her. He hadn't killed it after all!

Elation was heady and brought with it a crazy idea to test her theory. Dared she? Before she made a conscious decision, her feet were already moving. Closing the distance between them, she continued to slowly smooth her hair with her hands. She felt totally wanton as she set about blatantly seducing him. Never in her life had she taken the initiative like this, and her body stirred as a strange new excitement coursed through her veins. He was still watching her, as if mesmerised, and she knew that she had to make what she intended to do seem totally natural and unplanned.

Halting a yard away, she smiled at him before reaching for the spare towel and dabbing at the excess of moisture on her skin. Fascinated, she saw a nerve tick in his jaw as he followed the movement.

'Mmm, the water's marvellous,' she declared huskily, striving for a nonchalance she was light-years from feeling. Her eyes dropped to the dewed can Morgan held. 'Is this mine?' She took it from him easily, lifting it to rub it against her hot cheeks before carrying it to her lips and drinking deeply. 'Wonderful,' she breathed. Morgan's eyes rested on her lips, and at once they tingled as if he had actually touched them. Automatically the tip of her tongue slipped out to moisten them and she saw his hands ball into fists at his side.

Morgan took a deep breath that expanded his chest, drawing her eyes to the tanned expanse with its mat of dark, silky hair. 'Actually, that was mine. I put yours in the bag to keep cool,' he told her in an oddly strained voice, as if his control was being sorely tried.

Leigh hoped it was. She handed back the can with a curve of her lips. 'Oops! Sorry.' Dropping the towel, she reached for the tube of sunscreen. Squeezing some into her palm, she slowly began to smooth it over her arm. 'It must be close to lunchtime. Are you hungry yet?' she asked innocently.

The can crumpled in his hand with a sound like a pistol shot. They both looked at it, then Morgan tossed it irritably aside. 'No,' he said shortly.

She pulled a face and went to work on her other arm. 'Neither am I. It's too hot for food.' Oh, God, how long could she keep this up? Inside she felt all quivery and molten. Seducing him was sending her own senses crazy! She held out the tube to him. 'Do my back for me, would you?'

He took it. How could he refuse when he had been putting the cream on for two weeks? Yet, she was intensely aware of his reluctance. Not meeting his eyes, she quickly lay down on her stomach, resting her head on her arms. She held her breath as she heard him kneel down beside her. She felt as if she were on fire, her blood at boiling-point. At the first touch of his hand on her back, she sank her teeth into her bottom lip and stifled a moan. The glide of his hand down the entire length of her spine was a refinement of torturing pleasure, and her stomach clenched on a painful tug of desire.

She was glad she didn't have to speak, because she knew she couldn't have uttered a word. Morgan released the catch of her bandeau and began to smooth the cream over her ribcage, fingers brushing the swell of her breasts. She closed her eyes on a shudder of pleasure as, hidden, her nipples hardened into painful peaks that longed for his touch. He was using both hands now, with no pretence of merely applying cream. Each movement was a stroking caress of her silky skin, and it was driving her mad. She had never felt so aroused. She ached with need and longing, and didn't know how she could remain still another second.

The problem was taken out of her hands, for Morgan went still. So still, she could feel the imprint of each fingertip. She swallowed and waited. It seemed as if a lifetime had passed when he moved again to refasten her bandeau, but it could only have been seconds. She half turned then, and saw him sitting there, hands balled on his thighs.

'Shall I do your back now?' she asked as lightly as she could, desperate to hide her sense of triumph at the dull colour in his cheeks.

The look he threw her was fierce and she knew he knew what she had done. 'No. I'm going for a swim,' he gritted through a tight-clenched jaw and got abruptly to his feet. Seconds later, she heard the splash as he dived in.

Leigh collapsed back on to the towel, the knowledge tingling along her veins. Morgan wasn't immune to her at all. He still wanted her. Just what she would do with the knowledge, she had no idea, but for now it was enough just to know.

It was some time before Morgan returned to fling himself face-down on his own towel. He said nothing and kept his head averted. Leigh turned her head so that she could watch him. Did he feel as frustrated as she did? Even as she thought it, he turned his head and their eyes met. The naked longing in the blue depths made her catch her breath.

'You were going to do my back,' he murmured gruffly.

'Yes,' she said breathlessly, knocked completely off balance by this turn of events. Something must have happened to him while he was out there swimming, for his guard had disappeared completely. Subtly the control had changed hands. She sat up and reached for the tube with hands that trembled, then crawled across to kneel over him.

A very large lump lodged itself in her throat as she squeezed a dollop on to his back and began to rub it in. She had done this countless times, distancing herself from the act in her mind out of necessity, but now it was impossible. His skin was supple, like velvet, with planes that delighted her. Heart tripping madly, Leigh bit her lips as she caressed and explored him, delighting in the feel of his muscles contracting beneath her touch. It was incredibly sensual and arousing. So much so that, just as Morgan had done, she was forced to stop.

Digging her nails into her palms, she crawled away again. Sitting on her towel, she buried her face against her updrawn knees.

'Leigh.' Her name was soft and husky on his lips, and she had to look at him. His eyes burned her. 'Now we both know how it feels.'

She had to moisten dry lips. 'I——'

'You should have left well enough alone. It's dangerous to play with fire. I should have known you wouldn't be able to resist striking the match. A wise animal would run, but there's nowhere for you to run, is there?'

A *frisson* of fear chased through her. 'I don't know what you mean.'

A faint smile curved his lips. 'I know, but you will,' he declared huskily and lay down again.

Shaken off balance, she lay down. Her brain whirred madly. Oh, God, what did he mean? Could he possibly be saying that...? No! She mustn't think about it. He was playing a game she was unfamiliar with and she must wait and see. The ball was in his court now, but the rules had changed.

Nerves in a turmoil, she needed sheer effort of will to relax, but she did eventually, and soon the soporific effects of the sun made her fall asleep. When she woke, it was late afternoon.

'I thought you were never going to wake up,' a huskily amused voice declared, and she rolled on to her side to find Morgan resting on his elbow, watching her.

The warmth in his eyes was unsettling, and she felt awkward and shy to realise he had been watching her while she slept. It was as if someone had pulled the rug out from under her feet. She needed to know where she stood now. 'Morgan——'

She wasn't allowed to finish. 'Let's have another swim before we have to go back.' He was on his feet nimbly, reaching down a hand to her. She hesitated, eyes searching his, then placed her hand in his with a fatalistic sigh.

'All right,' she agreed, and was pulled to her feet. The movement brought her into contact with the whole length of him and she lost her breath on the sudden shock to the senses. He steadied her with his free hand, allowing it to run down her hip. He laughed as she was unable to stop a shiver, and released her, using only one hand to pull her after him to the water. He only let her go to dive into the waves. Leigh followed him, already so far out of her depth that she was unable to fight his deliberate teasing.

They swam for half an hour, and then collected their belongings and went back to the bungalow. Leigh was excruciatingly conscious of the hand he rested on her hip, and wondered just what she had unleashed. Morgan used the bathroom first, emerging in a very few minutes with a towel wrapped precariously around his hips and drying his hair with another.

He caught her eyes on him and smiled. 'It's all yours,' he said huskily, and watched her eyes widen.

'P-pardon?' Surely he couldn't mean...?

'The bathroom,' he enlarged, and burst out laughing as colour flooded her cheeks.

This new, improved Morgan was too much for Leigh. She scuttled into the bathroom and bolted the door with a sigh of relief. Her whole world had turned topsy-turvy in the space of an afternoon. She had roused the sleeping tiger and now discovered the jungle was a dangerous, unknown quantity.

Standing under the cool shower returned some of her calm. The trouble was that she had known exactly where she stood with an antagonistic Morgan. Even with a brotherly Morgan. Morgan the lover was something else. She mistrusted this sudden change of heart, was afraid to believe in it in case he should hurt her. Yet she knew she wouldn't go back to how it had been for all the money in the world. What a crazy, mixed-up fool she was!

When dropped in the deep end, the only course to take was to swim.

With that in mind, she lovingly smoothed her favourite body lotion on to her skin. Then, wrapped in a bathsheet, she padded back into the bedroom. Morgan had gone, she discovered, much to her relief. She dried her hair and applied a light make-up before going to contemplate her wardrobe. Give her mother her due, she certainly knew her clothes. Leigh was spoilt for choice. Finally she decided on a soft white jersey dress with a blouson top held up by thin straps. It flattered her tan, and only needed a pair of lacy panties underneath. Slipping into a pair of strappy white sandals, she sprayed Ivoire on to her pulse-spots, and was ready.

Morgan was waiting for her on the veranda, casually dressed in cream pleat-front trousers and a short-sleeved blue silk shirt. He turned as he heard her approach and they stared at each other in silence.

'Well, will I do?' she asked softly, shyly.

He came over to her, hand reaching out to cup her cheek, fingers probing the sensitive skin behind her ears. 'You look...beautiful,' he responded throatily. 'Very, very sexy.'

Leigh took in a shaky breath as all the hairs seemed to stand up on her body. 'Shall we go?'

They dined on the terrace overlooking the bay. Morgan kept up a flow of small talk that Leigh did her best to respond to lightly. She was very much aware that it wasn't their usual table, that Morgan must have asked for this romantically secluded one specifically. It sent her thoughts winging in all sorts of crazy directions. It was an effort to keep her feet on the ground.

Afterwards he took her hand and led her down to the beach. Leigh bent to remove her sandals, and Morgan took them from her. Slowly they began walking back towards the bungalow. Well away from the hotel, with only the moon to light their path, he turned her towards him, hands gently caressing her shoulders.

'Why, Morgan?' she asked softly, trying to hold back a shiver at the way his touch was making her feel.

Morgan looked down at her, eyes caressing her face. 'Why what?'

Nervous fingers combed her hair. 'You've changed your mind, and I don't understand why.' And she had to know.

He laughed under his breath. 'Is it absolutely necessary that you should?'

'Yes.' She nodded. 'Yes, it is.'

He smiled. 'I realised something today. I didn't know why I was fighting wanting you any more.'

Hastily she dropped her eyes, not wanting him to see how much of a blow that was. He was talking of wanting, not loving. To Leigh, the one was inextricably linked with the other, but it wasn't so for Morgan. She had hoped... Her head lifted.

'Because you've changed your mind about me?' she probed.

Morgan raised her hand. 'Because I see no reason why we should deny ourselves what we both want. You want me, and you know I still want you. You proved it very cleverly this afternoon,' he said drily, kissing her palm.

Heat invaded her cheeks, and she was thankful for the darkness. 'I also happen to love you,' she reminded him.

He shrugged. 'I didn't ask you to,' he came back evenly.

Her lips twisted. 'And you don't want it, right? You've just discovered that it's convenient, being married, to have your cake and eat it!' she sniped, trying to pull free.

Morgan easily thwarted her. 'Don't pretend you aren't hungry for cake too.'

How could she? 'It isn't supposed to be like this,' she cried despairingly.

His fingers tightened. 'But it's the way it is. I warned you about the fire.'

The fire of desire, not love! 'I don't want it!'

He expelled a mocking breath. 'It's too late for that. But I'll give you one last chance. Tell me to stop and I'll never touch you again. Never. Is that what you want, Leigh?' His gaze held her captive.

Leigh went utterly still. There she had it. If she said yes, she would lose him. The idea was frightening. He knew as well as she did that she didn't have the strength to turn him away. This had to be better than nothing, didn't it? She made the only choice that made sense.

'No. No, it isn't.' Her voice was soft, barely audible above the gentle sound of the waves. Please, she prayed, don't let me regret this.

'Then let's go,' he said gruffly, and reached for her hand.

She went with him, knowing this could be the way to more heartache than she had ever known. Yet her heart was racing like a trip-hammer when finally they stood in the privacy of their lounge.

Morgan turned to her then, lifting his hands to cup her face, thumbs gently caressing her cheeks. She could feel the tremble in them, as if he too was awed by this moment, and she moved her head the tiniest fraction to press a kiss to his palm. She felt his lips brush across her closed lids, her cheek, and then they were moving over hers almost reverently, once, twice, and lifted again.

There were wild storms in his eyes that were barely leashed as he looked at her. 'Dear God, I've wanted you for so long,' he confessed thickly.

The passion in his voice raised all the silky hairs on her flesh. She had waited for this moment all her life, and now it was here her emotions overwhelmed her. 'I've always been yours, always,' she whispered hoarsely.

With a groan he took her mouth again. Not gently this time, but with a passion that parted her lips to the sensual invasion of his tongue. It was as if he had lit a torch inside her and now she were going up in flames. Her head fell back as his lips left hers to plunder the sensitive cord of her neck, making her gasp in a shivering delight. His hands easily brushed aside the straps of her dress, and it fell away to her waist, revealing the aroused fullness of her breasts. Heavy lids fell over her eyes as his hands took their weight, thumbs circling the jutting peaks until they hardened. And then his mouth closed first on one and then the other, suckling and teasing, arousing a delirium of the blood that made her moan low down in her throat.

Morgan sank to his knees as lips and hands smoothed her dress down and away. The nerves in her belly fluttered and clenched as his mouth traversed its velvet swell, and she thought she would die when he pressed a kiss to the subtle V of her thighs through the sheer lace of her last flimsy covering.

'Morgan!' Her voice broke, and she swayed on legs so weak they barely held her upright. He looked up, and molten green eyes met explosive blue ones.

The next instant he was on his feet, eyes holding hers as he tore at the buttons of his shirt and shrugged it off. Then he was reaching for her, pulling her into his arms. Leigh arched against him, aching breasts seeking relief against the hardness of his chest, only to be teased by the silken mat of hair. Almost blindly, their lips sought each other until they met and engaged in a breathless battle.

With a groan, Morgan swept her into his arms and carried her through to the bedroom. He laid her gently on the bed, sliding away her last remaining covering, then feverishly removed the rest of his clothes before joining her, his long, powerful body coming down on hers satisfyingly. The feel of firm male flesh against her softness sent her senses spinning dizzily into space. His hands scorched her as they travelled every inch of her, each intimate caress sending her ever more wildly out of control. Yet she knew she was having the same effect on him, for as her hands explored the slick planes of his back and hips Morgan shuddered and moaned, and sought her lips in a kiss that drove them careering towards the edge of control.

So lost were they in the delights each brought the other that for a while neither of them heard the buzz of the telephone. Finally, though, it penetrated Morgan's consciousness and he went still with a disbelieving groan. It took Leigh a while longer to become aware of the noise, then she met his eyes in an agony of frustration. Morgan groaned again, dropping his forehead to hers.

'I'd better answer it,' he muttered thickly.

Leigh swallowed. 'Must you?'

Raising his head, he pulled a wry face. 'It doesn't sound as if they're going to give up. Stay right there. I'll be back.'

She watched him leave the bed and stride through to the lounge to lift the receiver that was still insistently buzzing. 'Yes...? Who...? Yes, I'll take it... Rose? What's wrong?'

Rose? At the name, Leigh quickly scrambled from the bed and reached for her robe, knowing the only reason the housekeeper would telephone was because something was seriously wrong. There was a tremor to her fingers as she tied the belt and went to join Morgan. Her heart contracted as she saw his grim expression. Still listening intently, Morgan looked at her. The distress she saw made her eyes widen, and he held out his arm. She slipped under it, putting both arms around his waist as his arm tightened on her shoulder.

'It's all right, Rose. Don't worry. We'll be there as soon as we can.' He said goodbye and slowly replaced the receiver.

Leigh looked up at him anxiously. 'It's Ralph, isn't it?'

Morgan's jaw tensed. 'Yes. He collapsed yesterday. Dr Radcliffe suggested we come home.'

'Oh, God!' She buried her face in his shoulder. 'He can't die, not Ralph!' she whispered. He had been her rock so long, it was unthinkable. 'What happened?'

Comfortingly, one hand stroked her hair. 'It was his heart. We'll know more tomorrow.'

Leigh desperately wanted to cry, but she knew that Morgan had enough to cope with. She could do more to help him by being practical. 'How are we going to get home?' she asked, and eased herself away, wiping the suspicion of moisture from her eyes.

There was a mixture of approval and something warmer in his eyes. 'I'll telephone the desk. Someone there will know what we can do,' he declared, reaching for the receiver again.

She nodded. 'While you do that, I'll pack a case. They can send the rest of our things on to us.'

'Leigh.' His soft use of her name stopped her in the bedroom doorway. 'Thanks.'

'I love him, too,' she replied huskily and passed through the door.

It didn't take long to pack a case with all they would need for the trip, then she gathered up clean underwear, jeans and a sweater and headed for the bathroom. Emerging ten minutes later, she was reaching for a pair of trainers when Morgan walked in.

'We're in luck. If we leave now by helicopter, we can just connect with a flight to New York. We'll go home from there.'

She went to him quickly, reading his tension despite his efforts to hide it. She took his hand and cradled it against her cheek. 'We'll be in time. I know we will.'

She thought for a moment he was going to pull his hand away, for he gave her the queerest look. Yet he didn't. Blue eyes searched hers for an aeon before he bent and pressed a soft kiss to her lips. 'You constantly confound me. Right this moment, Una would be running in the opposite direction. She never could abide illness.'

Leigh sighed. 'I know, but I'm not my mother.' How many times did she have to tell him?

Momentarily his face softened. 'I'm beginning to re-alise that for myself.' He moved away to the bathroom, halting in the doorway to look at her. 'I've been wrong about other things too. This is the wrong time and place, but some time soon I think you and I ought to have a talk.'

Bemused, Leigh watched the door close. Had he really said that? The frantic beat of her heart told her she wasn't dreaming. A warmth curling about her heart, she forced herself not to read too much into it. She had made that mistake before. This time she was going to be more cautious. Even so, deep inside, her heart was praying he meant what she thought he did.

CHAPTER NINE

LEIGH turned off the shower and stepped out of the cubicle, reaching for a large fluffy towel to wrap herself in. Wearily she sank on to the edge of the bath, and began to dry her hair with a hand towel.

'Let me do that.' Morgan's feet came into view, then his hands took the towel from her and began to rub gently.

Too tired to argue, and more than a little bemused by the novelty of it, she let herself be pampered. It felt marvellous, but not even that could wipe out the events of earlier that day. 'Why didn't he tell us?' she asked huskily.

Morgan's hands faltered momentarily, then went on. 'I don't know. Perhaps he didn't want us to worry. Perhaps he hoped he'd go quickly.' There was pain in his own voice.

Silently Leigh agreed the latter was most likely, but it hadn't worked out that way. They had driven straight to the hospital from the airport, to discover Ralph was in Intensive Care, his condition stable. Then the doctor had arrived to have a word with them, stunning them both with his assumption that they had known that Ralph had been diagnosed as only having a few months to live. When he realised they didn't know, he was most apologetic, explaining the situation with sympathy. Ralph had survived this attack but it was highly unlikely that he would survive another. The outcome was inevitable; it was only a matter of time now.

That had been an hour or more ago. Since then they had driven home in shocked silence, to be greeted by a tearful housekeeper who had had to be told the truth of her employer's condition. Leigh had found that the hardest to bear, for the elderly woman was more a part of the family than an employee. In the end, Morgan had taken control, sending her upstairs to their room—the master bedroom, last occupied when Morgan's mother was alive. A lot of care and attention had gone into getting it ready for them, but she was in no state to appreciate it.

Her own tears had been shed under the stinging spray of the shower, leaving her exhausted, both emotionally and physically. The journey home had been a nightmare of tensed nerves. The shock that followed their arrival found her at her weakest. Now she wanted to sleep but didn't know if she could.

'Rose said she'd bring up a tray of tea and sandwiches,' Morgan said now as he abandoned the towel, testing her hair with his fingers.

Leigh's senses stirred at his touch and she couldn't stop a tiny shiver of reaction. Eyes closing, she said, 'She shouldn't have bothered.'

'I imagine she feels better with something to do. You should try and eat something, it will make you feel better too,' he advised, framing her face with his hands to tip her head up.

'How can I eat at a time like this?' Leigh protested with a groan.

'Making yourself ill won't help Dad now, Leigh,' Morgan contested, studying her pale face and tired eyes. Letting her go, he bent and swept her up into his arms as if she weighed no more than a feather. 'Come on, let's get you into bed.'

He deposited her on the bed with a gentleness that brought a lump to her throat, held the covers while she slipped out of the towel, and then tucked them securely round her. He hovered over her, and Leigh felt sure he was about to kiss her when a tap on the door made him straighten up. It was Rose with a tray, and Morgan swiftly relieved her of it.

'Thanks a lot, Rose. You'd better get along to bed now. We'll be fine.'

Rose twisted her hands together. 'If you're sure then, Mr Morgan. You will let me know if...'

'As soon as we hear anything, we'll tell you. Try not to worry. Goodnight, Rose,' Morgan reassured her kindly.

With a nod, the housekeeper wished them both good-night and closed the door. Morgan set the tray down, poured a cup of tea and brought it over to Leigh with a plate of sandwiches.

'Drink this, and try to eat something. It will help you relax.'

'What about you?' Leigh asked as she obediently sipped at the steaming liquid and nibbled at a sandwich.

'I had something downstairs earlier. Right now, I'm going to shower. I won't be long.'

Leigh drank her tea, managing two sandwiches, and felt better for it. Setting cup and plate on the bedside table, she switched off the light and lay down. She felt leaden with weariness, but sleep had never seemed so far away. Closing her eyes, she lay listening to the sound of the shower. It was hypnotic, but it ended before she could slip over the edge into sleep.

She heard Morgan come in a little later, and felt the mattress sink as he lay down beside her and switched off the light. She had imagined he thought she was asleep, but realised he knew she wasn't when he reached out a long arm and pulled her round into the curve of his body. Her head came to rest on his shoulder, her hand on his chest.

'Relax, Leigh,' he ordered huskily. 'Go to sleep.'

That was all it took. With a little sigh, her eyes closed and she knew no more.

She was dreaming that she was lying on the beach. Her body was being deliciously warmed by the sun, cush-ioned by the moulding softness of the sand—and crabs were nipping at her fingers. Frowning, she tried to move away, but that only made them pinch harder. She gasped—and instantly woke up.

Her eyelids flickered open and made a discovery. It was Morgan's body keeping her warm, and which her own limbs were curved around. The crabs were his teeth as he nipped gently at the hand he had lifted to his lips. Seeing her awake, he stopped, eyes warm and sultry as he watched the colour rise in her cheeks.

'Good morning,' he greeted, voice low and husky.

Her heart jerked, and she let her gaze flicker to the window. 'It's still dark outside!' she exclaimed in soft surprise.

'Mm-hmm,' Morgan agreed as he deftly rolled her on to her back and took his weight on his elbows. Her heartbeat started to escalate as she saw the look in his eyes. 'I couldn't wait for you to wake up any longer.'

Her throat closed over. 'Oh.' It was a soft sound that could have meant anything. She was intensely aware of the heat coming from him as his arms effectively trapped her where she lay. But she had no intention of trying to escape. Each breath she took brought her breasts dangerously close to his bare chest, and she could feel her body responding to that nearness.

'I've been lying here for an hour wanting you. Can't you feel it?' he declared thickly, and his eyes reflected the flames that burnt in him.

She could feel it. Her own roused desire mirrored it. The air between them became charged with an elemental energy that made her shiver in the grip of an intense excitement. Her breathing went haywire, and stopped altogether as she watched his hot gaze shift to where her breasts were rising and falling rapidly. Pure instinct made her arch against him in mute invitation.

Morgan raised his eyes to hers again, cheeks stained a dull red. He moved, and she could feel the strength of his arousal. Her senses rioted, going wildly out of control as, with a muffled groan, he brought his mouth down on hers in a devastatingly sensual invasion. There was no gentle seduction. One touch and they were both at the same point, both wildly out of control. Morgan captured her head with his hands, holding her while he completed his ravishment of her mouth, and she revelled in it, returning the kiss with an instinctive sensuality.

They had always been an explosive combination, and now there was nothing to stop them. Her hands moved to his back, feeling his muscles clench at her touch, his strong body shuddering as she traced the line of his spine. The knowledge of her power exploded exultantly in her brain. She gloried in the freedom to explore his body, rediscovering its male beauty, delighting when he abandoned her lips to plunder her throat and she could hear his groans of pleasure, his words of encouragement.

With an impatient movement, he thrust the covers aside and seemed to freeze as he gazed down at her lissom body gleaming in the pale light. She watched him from beneath lowered lids, her breathing restricted as his hand came to take possession of her breast. A moan escaped her, and Morgan lowered his head to the perfumed valley of her breasts.

'You are *so* beautiful,' he muttered thickly.

He made her feel beautiful too, as his lips and hands worshipped her body, bringing the satin skin to pulsating life. Her fingers threaded into his hair as his mouth closed on first one breast and then the other, rousing the nipples to aching nubs with tongue and teeth. He was driving her crazy and, with a desperate moan, she clenched her fingers into the springy locks and tugged his mouth back to hers.

Their need was explosive, every kiss and caress hurtling them further and further out of control. There was no past or future, only the intensity of now that made their breath catch in painful delight, and their glistening bodies lock in a frenetic tangle of limbs.

Passion burned with a brightness and ferocity that couldn't be contained for long. It drove them on towards the final conflagration. When Morgan parted her thighs, Leigh gasped at the joy of his thrusting possession, her brief moment of pain passing as quickly as his hesitation. But there could be no stopping now, and they both knew it. She cried out as the coil of tension exploded inside her, and her nails dug into the flesh of his shoulders as he too climaxed with a long shudder of pleasure.

Slowly Leigh drifted back from that golden shore, so utterly complete for the first time in her life that she didn't mind Morgan's weight on her. She knew now that what they had just shared was totally right, and her heart swelled with all the love she felt for him. Only with Morgan could she feel this. She wanted to tell him, but sleep was sweeping over her, and she didn't have the energy to hold it back. Then Morgan eased his weight from her, moving on to his back, taking her with him to nestle close into his side as he reached for the covers. Giving up the unequal fight, she slept.

It was light when she was awakened by the warm glide of Morgan's hand along her thigh. It curved over her hip and waist, making her breath catch as his fingers curved possessively about her breast. Never had she been roused from sleep by such glorious sensations as his magical hands produced. Her senses stirred to life in an instant, and she lifted her head, lips reaching for his as he eased her to lie on top of him, hands gliding down to cup her hips.

This time their lovemaking was slower, more sensuous, taking them to even greater delights. Morgan's control was phenomenal as he brought her time and again to the brink of fulfilment, only to deny her—deny the both of them—that desired release. Finally, when she was writhing helplessly in his arms, he let go the bounds of his own need, and ended the delicious misery he had brought her to. From far away she heard her own voice crying out his name as she was hurtled into a kaleidoscopic explosion of passion.

They slept again.

Leigh awoke in the morning to a new and luxurious feeling of languor. She smiled to herself as memories of the night came back to her. It had been a revelation. No dream could ever have come close to the reality of what they had shared. A conviction that had flitted through her mind in the early hours took a firmer hold on her heart. Morgan couldn't have made love to her so beautifully without feeling something, she was sure. There had been something more than plain desire in the way he had held and caressed her. Something almost reverent. She believed she could put a name to it, but superstition kept it locked in her heart.

She didn't need to turn to know she was alone in the big bed, but even as it occurred to her to wonder where Morgan was he came in from the bathroom, a towel draped around his hips, his dark hair still damp from the shower. He must have felt her eyes on him for he stopped and looked across to the bed. It was impossible to hold back her feelings, and her smile was luminescent. It brought a strange expression flickering across his face momentarily, then it was gone. Crossing the floor to lower himself on to the bed beside her, he smiled.

'Good morning,' he greeted softly. 'How do you feel?'

After last night there was no room for shyness. 'Marvellous,' she responded honestly.

Blue eyes registered amusement. 'Hmm.' But that soon disappeared and he became serious. 'Why didn't you tell me it was the first time for you?'

Leigh couldn't stop the faint colour entering her cheeks. 'I didn't think it was important. Did I disappoint you?'

The broad chest expanded as Morgan took a deep breath. 'There was never any chance of that. When you give, you hold nothing back, do you?' His lips curved wryly. 'If I'd known I could have been gentler. Or tried. It's not easy to remain in control when you respond so beautifully. Did I hurt you?'

Leigh shook her head. 'No, you were wonderful.'

For the first time she saw Morgan a little disconcerted by her replies. He laughed oddly, shaking his head. 'You're very honest. So, why me, Leigh?'

'Don't you know?' She angled him a teasing look. 'It's really very simple, you know. I couldn't make love to anyone unless I loved them, and as I've only ever loved you...' She waited then with a fast-beating heart for what he would say to that. Always before he had rejected her declaration of love.

Morgan was frowning, and seemed to have difficulty finding words. 'What can I say?' he said huskily. 'You've given me a gift I wasn't expecting, a very precious one. I thought I knew you, but you're not at all what I expected. You continually surprise me.'

It was so unusual to see the proud, confident Morgan unsure that she almost laughed. It was going to be all right, every instinct told her so. Leigh tilted her head and smiled provocatively. 'Don't you like surprises?'

Lights flickered in his eyes as he surveyed her. 'Only the right ones,' he conceded with a laugh.

Her confidence grew in leaps and bounds. She laughed too, a husky sound way down in her throat. 'Then I must make sure I only give you the right ones.' To see him so relaxed was a joy in itself.

Morgan crossed his arms over his chest and raised an eyebrow. 'You're getting very adventurous all of a sudden.'

Her eyes locked with his. 'I've wanted to be, but this is the first time you've ever let me. I don't think you realise how happy you've made me. These last few weeks I've been lonely, waiting for you to let me in. God, it was so cold out there on my own.' She had spoken from the heart, and the instant it was said she felt him withdraw from her, mentally, if not physically. Her heart knocked anxiously. 'What's wrong?'

Morgan frowned. 'I find your honesty—uncomfortable. It isn't easy to accept responsibility for someone else's happiness. I don't know that I can ever give you what you want.'

Her eyes clouded. She knew what he meant. 'Because you can never look at me and not see my mother,' she stated flatly, trying to keep the bitterness from her voice, but knowing she had failed by the sharp look he sent her. 'I'm sorry, but I don't know what I can do about the way I look.'

His sigh was heavy. 'The fault isn't yours, it's mine. Right now, you've got me as mixed up as I ever hope to be. I want to believe I've been wrong, but I keep coming up against the spectre of Una. Unless I can get over that, there is no future for us. I'll make you no promises that I can't keep. This is a problem I'll have to deal with in my own way. I can try to overcome it, but if I'm to be as honest as you, then you have to know that I don't know if I can.'

She had to respect his honesty, however bitter the reality. But there was something she had to know. 'Do you want to try? Be honest a little longer. Don't allow me to hope, if it isn't what you really want.' All her life, it seemed, she had lived in her mother's shadow. To have to lose Morgan because of it now would be too cruel. Everything she had ever wanted was within her grasp— fate couldn't deal her such a crippling blow at the eleventh hour.

Once again Morgan sighed. 'All I know for certain is that I want you more than I've ever wanted any woman. That the prospect of losing you is too bitter to contemplate. What I feel is a stronger emotion than I ever imagined I could experience. With honesty I can't say more.'

It was more than she expected and less than she hoped, but she accepted it. For now it was enough to go on with. To push might lose her everything, when just a little patience would win the battle.

'I can live with that, only promise me one thing. If it's to be no, then tell me quickly, for kindness' sake.'

He nodded gravely. 'You have my word.'

Leigh gave a little sigh and sat up. She pulled the sheet up over her breasts and anchored it with her hand. 'Have you phoned the hospital this morning?'

Morgan seemed relieved at her change of subject. 'I rang first thing. He's stable and awake. We can go in whenever we like.'

Leigh immediately forgot her own disappointment in a rush of relief. Her smile blossomed. 'Oh, thank God!'

The exclamation was heartfelt. 'I'll get up now, and we can go straight after breakfast.'

Morgan caught her arm as she made to clamber out the other side. 'Don't forget, this is only a temporary reprieve, Leigh,' he warned.

'I haven't forgotten. I'm just glad of this chance to say goodbye properly. I want us all to make the most of the time he has left. I hate the thought of him dying alone,' she replied huskily. Her nerves leapt in response as Morgan leant forward and brushed his lips lightly over hers.

'You've a kind heart, Leigh Fairfax. Do you take in stray animals too?'

Leigh kept her tone as light as his. 'Of course. They know they can trust me. And if shy, nervous creatures can do that, it must be easier for a wary, distrustful human.'

His brows rose. 'Meaning me?'

Leigh shrugged. 'If the cap fits...' She left that hanging.

Reluctant humour danced across his face. 'Has anyone ever told you you're pushy?'

Laughing, she scrambled from the bed and reached for her robe. 'Not lately.' Tightening her belt, she crossed to the dressing-room to collect clean underwear. 'However,' she said as she re-emerged and headed for the bathroom, 'I don't have time to argue with you now, delightful though it is. The only man I'm interested in this morning is your father.'

Morgan stood up and took a step towards her. 'Is that so? It would be very easy for me to refute that statement.'

The look he gave her sent a delicious tingle up her spine. Any other morning she might have taken up the challenge, but not this one. 'You could, but you won't,' she declared, not bothering to hide her disappointment that it was the right place but the wrong time.

A fact he conceded with a sigh. 'No. I think I can spare you to my father for a little while. Go and shower, Leigh. I'll meet you downstairs.'

Leigh disappeared into the bathroom, wondering if Morgan realised how possessive he sounded. Probably not, but she hugged the knowledge to herself, greedy for any signs that said he cared. It had been a long dark tunnel, but now there was the faintest light at the end of it.

In the fickle way fate had of dealing her hands, the illness that was taking Ralph from them brought Leigh and Morgan closer together.

Nothing was said of the conversation they had had as the days went by. Morgan had to fight this battle on his own, she had no part in it, save to watch and wait—and hope.

Leigh had worried that life would revert to the way it had been now they were home, but it didn't. It was as if a wall had come down. She wondered if Morgan re- alised that he now actively sought her company, and that he would more often than not smile when he saw her. They were subtle things, but oh, so important to her in the light of what he had said. Because they came from within without thought, revealing how his vision of her had changed—was constantly changing.

The nights were perfect. Then he would reach for her and they would make love until they fell asleep in each other's arms, only to wake in the early morning light to make love again. But what she valued most in those days of waiting was to see him so relaxed and at peace beside her at the end of the day. Sometimes they would talk, at others listen to music, relaxed and comfortable, yet both aware of that elemental spark not far beneath the surface, just waiting for the right moment to ignite.

She responded to his moods, giving him the room he needed, and found satisfaction in his acceptance of it. She wondered sometimes, as she sat curled up beside him on the couch, if she realised it was love she was giving him in all its variations. Or that, in accepting it, he was acknowledging that love existed between them. Because he did love her, she was convinced of it in the depth of her heart where words were unnecessary.

It brought a glow to her that made Rose smile, and everyone else who saw her, because the cause of it was obvious to anyone with half an eye. But it was a bitter-sweet period. Always hanging over her was the threat of his losing the battle. Something she must be a constant reminder of, as her reflection told her. They were bitter-sweet days, too, because of Ralph.

They hadn't stayed long that first visit, for fear of tiring him. Instead they paid frequent short visits until his improvement restricted them to the normal visiting hours. It was hard to watch his slow recovery, having to temper relief with the knowledge that it was only temporary. That, however much better he looked, the strength was gone from him. More and more they knew it was only a matter of time.

In fact, they had Ralph for another two months before he passed away quietly in his sleep. The last five weeks he spent at home with them, both Leigh and Morgan had insisted on that. They were poignant weeks. Their unspoken determination to make Ralph's last weeks happy brought them closer still.

The end, when it came, was a shock, however much they had been expecting it. Grief took them differently. Leigh gave way to tears, turning to Morgan for comfort, but he remained stolidly in control. She watched un-happily as he dealt with the formalities with a grimly set face. She would almost have thought his reserve in-human if she hadn't seen the mask crack, revealing a devastating sorrow. Only for a moment did it last, then the shutters went up and he muttered a vague excuse about work and shut himself in the study.

For an hour she paced restlessly around the house, torn between her knowledge of the need Morgan had clearly stated to be alone, and her own conviction that at this time they needed each other more than ever. On the moving screen of her mind's eye she saw his haunted eyes, and came to a decision. He needed her, even if he was too proud to admit it. But she already knew how cold and lonely pride could be, and she wasn't going to leave him alone with it. She loved him too much.

Her feet beat a decisive tap-tap on the floor as she made her way to the study. She didn't knock, but went straight in. As she had suspected, Morgan wasn't working. He was standing staring out of the window, hands clenched on the frame. He looked round when he heard the door, and her breath caught as she saw the gleam of tears in his eyes.

But they were quickly dispelled by anger. 'Go away, Leigh,' he gritted thickly.

Her answer was to firmly shut the door, refusing to be cowed by his cold, angry face. 'No. I won't be shut out any more, Morgan.' Though her stomach churned, she crossed the room and slipped her arms around him. His rejection was palpable, and one hand came to pry hers free, but she staunchly resisted that, too. Swallowing hard, she rested her cheek against his rigid back. 'Please trust me, Morgan. I loved him too, remember. I can't believe he's gone. I miss him so. Please talk to me,' she urged in a husky, tender voice.

He remained silent so long, she thought she had failed, but then his fingers clenched so tightly about her own that she had to stifle a groan of pain. At first his words were a low rumble in his chest that she could scarcely make out, but they grew stronger and became a flood that was unstoppable. He didn't turn to look at her, so he couldn't see the silent stream that flowed down her own cheeks, nor the teeth that bit her lip hard to stifle her sobs as she listened to that outpouring of love.

Finally, with a deep sigh, he fell silent, toying with her fingers before lifting them gently to his lips. Even such a soft touch on her tender flesh made her gasp, and he turned at last, eyes widening as he saw the bruised hand and lip and the molten green of her eyes.

'Oh, love.' The words were soft, stricken with remorse as he released her only to put his arms about her.

Her own arms clung tightly as he buried his face in her hair. 'God, I'm sorry. I'm a selfish swine. I don't deserve you.'

'Yes, you do!' she protested with watery ferocity.

He groaned. 'I'm always hurting you.'

'But you don't really mean to.'

'Why do we always hurt those who deserve better of us? You came to offer me comfort and this is how you're rewarded. Why do you put up with it?'

'Because I'm not very bright. Besides, don't you know, you only hurt the ones you love?'

His hands moved to cup her cheeks and tip her face up to his. 'Leigh...' Her name was a moaned protest.

Green eyes beseeched his. 'I know you feel vulnerable, but so do I. It would be so very easy for you to hurt me—really hurt me—but I trust you not to. Can't you trust me to do the same for you?'

'If it were only that simple——' he began on a sigh.

'But it is,' Leigh interrupted instantly. 'You don't trust me, because you don't trust my mother. What I look like doesn't matter, it's what's inside that counts. Oh, Morgan, why can't you just close your eyes and trust your heart?'

'You dazzle me so that I want to do anything for you,' he groaned, and brought his mouth down on hers with a breathless passion that was over much too soon. 'My mind whirls with thoughts until I think I'll go mad. Yet when I'm with you everything seems sane. Everything clicks into place as if it was meant to be. But is it real?' he finished as one tormented.

Her eyes shone with a fierce light. 'If you can feel it, then it's real, Morgan. Believe in it, trust it. I promise it won't fade away.'

'God, how I want to believe you,' he declared, staring into her eyes for an answer to all his unspoken questions. Then with a guttural sound he swept her up into his arms, cradling her against his chest as he strode to the door. 'What I look at is real, and what I touch. With you in my arms I have no doubts. If it means I have to keep you there, then that's what I'll do, because I can't fight any more, Leigh. You've beaten me.'

Her heart cried out that she didn't want to beat him, but her voice was silent. She'd turn his defeat into victory so that he would never regret the choice he had just made. However long it took, she'd teach him that love was a beginning, not an end. Right now, though, they simply needed each other. Needed to feel the surge of life that the joining of their bodies brought, to chase away the spectre of death.

She clung to him, her face buried against his shoulder, and didn't protest as he carried her up to their room.

CHAPTER TEN

LEIGH stood beside Morgan in the churchyard, accepting the condolences of those people who had come to pay Ralph their last respects. A little way away, Una stood talking to the vicar. Unexpectedly, her mother had been just as shocked by her husband's death as they were, and it made Leigh wonder if perhaps she had cared for him rather more than she would have liked to admit.

Her eyes passed on to Morgan. In this past week, he had told her in all but words that he loved her. The words, she decided, weren't really important, not when you knew. He must have felt her eyes on him, for he turned and smiled at her briefly before his attention was claimed once more. She felt a glow start up inside her. She wanted to see him smile with that same slow warmth in his eyes when she told him her news.

The thought brought quite a different glow to life. How she could have gone so long without realising, she couldn't imagine, but it had only been this morning that she had discovered she was carrying Morgan's baby. She had thought of telling him at once, but something made her hesitate. It wasn't that she doubted he would be as delighted as she was, simply a need to keep it as her secret for a little longer. She decided to wait until the funeral was over to tell him. A day or two wouldn't make much difference now.

Una shared their car on the short drive back to the house, where she immediately monopolised centre stage, much to Leigh's dismay. Instinctively she sought Morgan out, trying to gauge his reaction to the manoeuvre, and was relieved to discover that he was ignoring it, or, at the very least, pretending to. Abhorring her mother's tendency to hog the limelight, Leigh also wished her timing could have been better. Right now, she didn't want Morgan drawing any more unfavourable similarities.

She heaved a heartfelt sigh of relief when the last of the mourners departed, some two hours later, but that only signalled the reading of the will. It was going to be one of the hardest parts of the day, and she had been dreading it. So far Morgan had been amazingly tolerant of his stepmother's presence, but she wondered just how long that would last once the contents of the will were divulged.

Humphrey Berridge, Ralph's solicitor, arrived after lunch. He was a rather pompous man, rotund and balding, whose ideas were firmly entrenched in the rightness of things. Which was why they gathered in the solemnity of the study rather than the ease of the lounge. Watching him arrange himself at the desk, Leigh caught Morgan's eye as he sat beside her, and had to bite hard on her lip as he raised his eyebrows expressively. For a moment the mood lightened, but faded as the solicitor went through the usual formalities and then began reading out the contents in what he no doubt considered a suitably solemn voice. Leigh's opinion was that it only made a bad situation worse. Having dealt with the minor bequests, he raised his head from the document and requested all but Morgan, Leigh and Una to leave the room.

'Mr Fairfax was most precise in his instructions,' Mr Berridge felt bound to elaborate once the room had cleared.

Una crossed one slim leg over the other crossly. 'Trust Ralph to be mysterious to the last!'

The solicitor smiled thinly. 'With your permission? As I told you over the telephone, your father, Mr Fairfax, had occasion to alter his will fairly recently.'

Morgan frowned faintly. 'I take it from that that it wasn't something he made a habit of. So how recently was it?'

'About three months ago, I believe. But let me say quite categorically that, although your father knew he was dying, he was in full possession of his faculties,' Mr Berridge declared severely.

'I'm sure he was,' Morgan agreed frostily. 'Or are you suggesting we may have cause to doubt it?'

The solicitor's face flushed. 'Certainly not!' he denied, affronted.

Morgan's smile was perfunctory. 'Then you'd better get on with it.'

Mr Berridge sighed and lifted the document. 'Your father was very precise in his wording of the main bequest. I shall therefore read it as he dictated it to me. "To my son, Morgan, I leave my house and the bulk of my estate—with one proviso. That his marriage to my stepdaughter, Leigh Armstrong, takes place and that the marriage be a firm and genuine commitment. It shall be judged to be so only by the production of an heir within two years. If, however, the marriage is dissolved before that time, or no child is born for other than sound medical reasons, the house and estate will revert to my stepdaughter, Leigh."

'"Finally, to my wife I leave my London apartment and all its contents, together with a lump sum of twenty thousand pounds, which, if invested wisely, should see her comfortably over the next few years. By which time, I am certain, she will have found a more secure future."'

The silence that heralded the last words was broken at last by a peal of amused laughter from Una.

'My God, the crafty old devil! Who ever would have thought it? On the whole I think I came out of it rather well. But you, darling!' She patted her daughter's rigid shoulder. 'I've always said, if you sow wisely, you reap a bumper crop. Congratulations on becoming a very wealthy woman!'

Leigh was already shaken by the will; Una's implications knotted her stomach. It wasn't the time for such jokes. 'Mother, please!' Leigh cast her parent an exasperated glance before turning to where Morgan sat in a stony silence. A chill of apprehension chased its way along her spine. Why didn't he say something, anything? She reached out a hand to touch his arm and the look he sent her was so scathing she withdrew it again on a gasp of alarm. My God, he couldn't believe what Una had implied! That it had all been a plot!

Humphrey Berridge cleared his throat. 'I take it there is nothing you wish me to explain?' Receiving only silence in reply, he gathered up his papers. 'In that case, I'll be on my way. Please don't hesitate to call me if the need arises.'

Una, glancing from her daughter to Morgan, rose gracefully to her feet. 'Do let me show you out, Mr Berridge. I have the feeling that at this moment, you and I are quite *de trop*.'

When the door closed behind them, Leigh turned a chalk-white face to Morgan, shivering as she met the bitter anger in his eyes. 'There has to be some mistake,' she declared hoarsely.

Morgan laughed bitterly. 'And I'm the one who nearly made it! Whose idea was it, Leigh? Yours or your mother's?'

Her fingers clenched on the wooden arms of the chair. 'Are you mad?' How could he even begin to think it? Hadn't he learnt to trust her?

Pure venom flashed from his eyes. 'No, not mad, nor a fool. First you trap me into this marriage, and now you're taking everything else!'

Leigh couldn't believe that in one fell stroke he was wilfully destroying all that they had built. She went cold. 'That's a lie, Morgan, and you know it,' she denied unevenly.

'Is it?' his lip curled. 'Did you think I was blind? Three months ago that will was drawn up. Exactly at the moment your mother turned up again. And what happened? First you and she get together for a cosy little chat, after which she gets to work on my father! Then, hey presto, he rushes off to town without a word of explanation. Well, we know why now, don't we? My God, there's nothing to compare with the fury of scorned women! I turn you both down and this is your idea of a perfect revenge!' He rose abruptly and strode to the window.

'I've never wanted revenge of any sort. Morgan, I swear to you that I had nothing to do with this,' she protested in a choked voice.

'Do you swear, too, that the subject of children was never, at any time, mentioned between you?' he shot back angrily.

'Yes, I . . .' The assertion died on her lips as she recalled the conversation she had had with her mother. Guilt must have been plastered across her face, and Morgan witnessed it. His expression was bleak. Her heart gave a painful kick. 'No, I can't, but——'

He interrupted her. 'Whose idea was it, Leigh?' he repeated in a voice so cold she winced.

Staring at him, she rose unsteadily to her feet. 'I can explain if you'll only——'

'Who?' His fist thumped on the window-frame.

Leigh swallowed painfully. 'She said——'

'So it was her!' Again he interrupted, giving her no chance. 'The conniving bitch!'

'I take it you're referring to me?' Una enquired in amusement.

Neither of them had heard her return, and they turned as one to the door. Leigh was the first to find her voice.

'Oh, God, Mother, what have you done?'

Una wandered to the nearest mirror and tweaked a few hairs back into place. 'Apparently got you a fortune. Although I must admit I wasn't entirely sure what Ralph had in mind.'

Leigh swallowed the lump of fury that threatened to choke her. Going to her mother, she jerked her away from her reflection with hard hands. 'How could you do it? How could you hurt me for mere spite?'

Una sent a daggers look at the silent man over her daughter's shoulder. 'Not you, darling. It was Morgan I wanted to hurt, and I have, haven't I?' she jeered.

Leigh shook her head incredulously. 'But you have hurt me, Mother, because I love Morgan. You knew that!' she exclaimed angrily.

'Darling, there are other men,' Una declared lightly, pulling herself free of Leigh's hands.

'Not for me!' Leigh cried. 'Never for me! Oh, God, I don't think I can forgive you for this! You'd better go. You've got what you wanted, seen what you came to see. Just leave us alone from now on.'

Una shrugged, not in the least disturbed by her daughter's outburst. 'Don't worry, I intend to go. This was never my favourite spot on the map. However, I won't mind visiting you from time to time in the future— once Morgan has moved out, of course. Ciao, darling.' She went from the room without a backward glance.

Abruptly, Leigh turned back to Morgan. He had taken the chair behind the desk. No longer angry, he looked pale and drawn. There was a fine tension in the set of his body. 'You can't still believe I had anything to do with this?' she challenged.

Morgan gave a deep sigh and rubbed a hand wearily around his neck. 'No. She made that pretty clear. The question is, where do we go from here?'

Her moment of relief had been brief, now alarm bells jangled wildly. 'What do you mean? It's obvious, isn't it?'

'Not to me. My father put the ball firmly in your court. What do you intend to do with it?'

Leigh frowned, reaching out an unsteady hand to hold on to the back of the nearest chair. 'Do? How can you ask that? *Why* do you ask it?'

A muscle flexed in his jaw. 'Because you could walk out of this house now a very wealthy woman. You don't need me or my family any more.'

'I don't believe I'm hearing this!' she gasped angrily. 'Don't need you? Doesn't anything get through to you? I'll always need you, Morgan, because I'll always love you. How often do I have to say it?'

There seemed to be a war going on inside him. A battle he was losing. It made his voice brusque when he said, 'If you weigh love against money, it doesn't balance, Leigh.'

Something in the way he said it made her go utterly still. She stared at him, doubting her own senses. 'Are you testing me?' she demanded to know in a low, disbelieving voice.

Morgan hesitated an instant before replying. 'I suppose I am,' he said slowly.

'I see.' She felt cold, cold to her heart. 'And what is this... test?' She spat the word out as if it were unclean.

His eyes quartered her pale, set face, then abruptly he rose to his feet, crossing to the window again, to stand there looking out, hands thrust into trouser pockets. 'Will you give me an heir?' he said harshly.

Leigh swayed. Automatically her hand rose to settle on her stomach as if to protect the tiny life that lay there. 'Why? So that you can come into your inheritance? Is that what you're saying, Morgan? Will I give you a child to prove I don't want your money?' She had never believed he could hurt her so much!

Morgan stiffened, squaring his shoulders before he turned to face her, and there was something dogged and unflinching in his set expression. 'Yes, that's what I'm saying. Will you do it?'

How dared he? She was so angry she was calm. 'No.' There were things she wouldn't hesitate to do for him, but in this she wasn't that self-sacrificing. He had picked on perhaps the only reason she would refuse to give him a child. 'No, Morgan. A thousand times no.'

For a moment there was an awesome silence, then his hands came from his pockets and balled into fists. 'So, it's the money you want, after all,' he declared harshly.

Deep inside her, something screamed. 'You can't really think that!'

He dragged a hand through his hair in a helpless gesture. 'What else am I to think? If you love me, you'll do it.'

It was a dagger-thrust to the heart, and she gasped. 'Let me get this right. Not only do I have to prove I don't want your money, now I have to prove I *love* you? My word isn't enough? That's the filthiest, most disgusting attempt at blackmail I've ever heard!' She closed her eyes for a moment, and when she looked at him again they were bleak. 'You know I can't refuse. How could I? It would make everything I'd ever said a lie. Congratulations, you've won. I hope it makes you very happy. Now, if you'll excuse me, I think I'll get some fresh air.'

Morgan called her name sharply as she went through the door, but she ignored him. She didn't think she could stand being in the same room as him a moment longer. Collecting a coat from the closet, she slipped it on and left the house.

She walked for miles, locked in a numb no man's land between anger and despair. She didn't know how long it would take for her to forgive him, or even if she could. One thing was clear—he didn't love her. How could he, and make that demand? Could her own love withstand this latest knock? Surely there must be a point at which it would break? Was this it? She was too numbed by shock to know. Perhaps it was a blessing in disguise, stopping her from feeling the pain of her breaking heart.

How she wished Ralph hadn't made that will. She knew he had had the best of motives. He had wanted to give her a secure future, but to Morgan it must have seemed like a betrayal. Perhaps she should be grateful that his reaction had pulled the wool from her eyes. Perhaps it *was* better to know the truth, but, dear heaven, had it had to hurt so much?

It was beginning to get dark when she made her way back home again, body tired and brain still thankfully numb. Not wishing to run into Morgan, Leigh went straight up to their room. She could tell from the cast-off clothes that he had been up to change for dinner. Never having felt less like food, she went through to the bathroom, drew a deep, hot bath, and sank into it with a sigh.

The warmth eased tired muscles and released the tension the day had brought. Only when the water had cooled right down did she climb out, drying herself on a large fluffy towel before slipping on her nightdress and going to bed.

When Morgan came in later, she was glancing through a magazine. It was impossible to ignore him. All her senses responded to his presence as they always had. Some things would never change. Steeling herself, she looked across at him, eyes unknowingly large in a pale face.

Morgan was standing just inside the door. She couldn't see his face for the one bedside lamp glowing scarcely lit more than a third of the large room. But she could sense his indecision, as if he wasn't sure just how to proceed from where they had left off. Then he moved, approaching the bed, and she saw the half-empty glass of whisky in his hand.

'Rose saved you some dinner,' he said uncomfortably.

'I wasn't hungry.'

'No.' He accepted that rather uneasily. He seemed about to say something, then changed his mind. 'Where did you go?'

Leigh shrugged. 'Here and there. I don't really remember, to tell you the truth. Is it important?'

Blue eyes regarded her steadily. 'I was worried about you. You could have been lying out there somewhere, hurt.'

'I'm sorry to have been the cause of concern. As you can see, it wasn't necessary,' she responded coolly.

Morgan compressed his lips. Once more he seemed on the verge of saying something, only to bite it back. Abruptly he turned away, swallowing down the remainder of his drink in one go. The glass slammed down on the chest of drawers as he passed on to the bathroom and disappeared inside.

Leigh hadn't realised just how tense she was until she let out a shaky breath. Slowly she closed the magazine and dropped it to the floor. Feeling returned with the grip of invisible fingers about her heart. Tears threatened, and she swallowed them back, reaching out to switch off her lamp, then lay down on her side, waiting.

She heard the shower go off, and not long afterwards Morgan padded silently back into the darkened room. The bed tilted under his weight as he climbed in beside her. Though she had expected him to reach for her, his touch on her bare arm was still a shock. Her body wanted to melt against him, to find oblivion in his lovemaking, but her heart and mind cried out against it. So, instead of melting, she froze.

'Don't touch me!' Her voice was full of a husky distaste, directed not just at him but herself as well.

Beside her, Morgan froze too, his fingers biting into her flesh. 'What?'

'I said, don't touch me,' she repeated evenly.

Silence followed, then the bed rocked as he moved and his lamp was switched on. A determined hand rolled her on to her back, and she found herself staring up into a set, angry face.

'What's going on, Leigh? This afternoon——'

'I said I had no choice,' she interrupted huskily. 'I didn't say I was willing to have you touch me again.'

He frowned heavily. 'What the hell does that mean?'

'Can't you guess?' she mocked, lips trembling as she held grimly on to her emotions. 'It means I'm already pregnant.'

To say Morgan was shocked was an understatement. 'Pregnant!' His eyes dropped to her body beneath the covers, and he pushed them back to lay his hand on her flat stomach, his touch so gentle she barely felt it. 'Darling, that's marvellous.'

Leigh gasped, tears burning her eyes. Angrily she brushed his hand away. 'Oh, yes! Now you know your damned inheritance is perfectly safe! Oh, God, how you make me sick!' She tried then to scramble from the bed, but Morgan was up on his knees in an instant, hands fastening with gentle force on her shoulders, stopping her.

'No! Leigh! Darling, don't.' His words came out choked.

She pressed her lips together as she subsided. 'Don't *darling* me. I'm not your darling. You proved that this afternoon!' she declared bitterly. Incredibly she felt his lips brush lightly over her hair.

'Oh, God! You don't understand!' Morgan murmured thickly.

'Oh, but I do. I understand only too well. Don't treat me like an idiot, Morgan!' Why couldn't he let her go? His hands were so soft and gentle they made her heart ache.

'Hell! I've made such a mess of it!' His voice was tortured.

She couldn't agree more. 'Let me go, Morgan. At least have the guts to stop pretending you care!'

Morgan groaned. 'But that's just it, darling, I do care. More than I've ever said.'

His hold had slackened, so that this time she managed to pull away from him. Turning, her eyes flashed at him. 'Oh, you care all right. After all, I'm giving you what you want.'

Morgan flinched. He would have touched her but she reared back from him. He slammed his fist on his thigh. 'Damn! Leigh, listen to me, you've got it all wrong. OK, I know that was my fault, but at least give me the chance to put it right. I'm trying to tell you I love you.'

She laughed. She took one look at his serious face, and it slipped out. But, having once started, she couldn't stop. It went on and on, echoing in her ears until the crack of Morgan's palm on her cheek shocked the breath from her. The tears that she had been holding back all day finally overflowed. With a wrenching sob, Leigh buried her head in her hands and gave in to her misery.

She didn't have the strength, or the will, to fight when Morgan pulled her into his arms, cradling her against his chest. He rocked her as if she were a baby, one hand smoothing rhythmically over her hair. Only when her sobbing slowly died away did she become aware that he had been talking too, in a low, intense voice.

'Oh, sweetheart, I'm sorry. Forgive me. I never meant to hurt you. Shush . . . hush now. God, I hate to hear you cry like this! Don't break your heart over me, I'm not worth it!'

They were just the words that got through to her, and she reacted to them instinctively. 'I'll be the judge of that!' she argued thickly.

Morgan froze, his hand stilling on her hair, then gently it tipped her face up to his. She drew in her breath when she saw the white, haunted face looming over her. 'I'm sorry,' he said again.

She felt limp, totally drained. 'Are you?' she asked flatly, unemotionally. She felt Morgan's chest rise and fall as he took a deep breath.

'You're exhausted. Why don't you lie down and get some sleep? We'll talk in the morning.'

Leigh was too tired to argue. She allowed Morgan to settle her back down and draw the covers over her. Her eyes felt gritty and heavy, and she closed them. She didn't feel the soft brush of his lips on her hair for she was already asleep. With a sigh, Morgan settled down beside her. Switching off the lamp, he lay back to wait out the night.

Leigh came awake with a start. Sunlight was streaming into the room. She didn't know what had roused her, but a glance at the clock told her it was about time anyway. She rubbed at her eyes. They felt stiff, and it was that which brought remembrance of the events of yesterday back to her. Morgan. The baby.

Cautiously she turned on to her back. He lay spread out beside her, hair tousled, chin shadowed by a growth of beard, and frowning faintly as he slept. His dreams, whatever they were, were troubled.

Leigh stared at him. Could he have meant what he said last night? Did he love her? She wanted to believe him. But if it was true, why had he attempted to blackmail her? It didn't make any sense. Dear heaven, she was so confused. He had said they would talk, and she wanted to shake him awake now and demand the answers to her questions. But she looked at his face, and saw the tiredness there. He looked as if he had lain awake all night and had only just fallen asleep. She bit her lip and knew she couldn't wake him.

She lay still, wishing Ralph were here. But Ralph was gone, and couldn't offer her his gentle wisdom. Yet, she realised, she could still talk to him, and suddenly she knew that was what she needed to do. Carefully, so as not to wake Morgan, she slipped from the bed, collected underwear, jeans and sweater, and padded into the bathroom to shower and change.

Ten minutes later she was letting herself out of the house and crossing the drive to where she had parked her car round the side of the house. It usually took some time to get the engine to fire, but this morning it wouldn't start at all. Thumping the steering-wheel, she released the bonnet and climbed out again to have a look. Before she could do anything, though, she heard a car coming up the drive, swinging to a gravel-crunching halt before the door.

Intrigued, she walked round to investigate, instantly recognising Toby's sporty car. He was just climbing out, and her smile blossomed as she crossed to him. Hearing her approach, he turned with a wave.

'Hi. I came over to see if you'd be interested in a ride this morning,' he greeted as they met, yet sounding rather uptight for her usually buoyant friend.

'Well actually I was going to drive down to the church, but my car wouldn't start,' Leigh explained, watching him curiously.

'No problem. I'll give you a lift. The church will be as good a place as any.'

Her brows rose. 'For what?'

Toby grinned. 'For what I have to say,' he declared sheepishly.

'Something's happened! It's Helen, isn't it? Don't tell me you finally plucked up the courage to propose?' she teased.

He laughed. 'I did, and she said yes.' His smile broadened even as he shook his head. 'I still can't believe it. She said yes.'

'Oh, Toby, I'm so happy for you!' Leigh cried, and flung her arms about his neck to hug him. Toby's arms took her own breath away.

'Thanks,' he said as they stood back, smiling warmly at each other.

Leigh couldn't have been more delighted. He was such a nice man, and Helen would make him the perfect wife. 'Come on, you can tell me all the details while you drive.'

Yet they had barely settled in their seats when a figure rushed from the house. It was Morgan. Jeans-clad, but otherwise bare, and seemingly oblivious of the sharp gravel beneath his bare feet, he ran towards them. Leigh had never seen him look quite so white and angry as he did when he yanked open her door and ordered her out.

'What?' She blinked dazedly up at him.

'I said, get out,' he gritted, and to underline the point very nearly pulled her bodily from the seat, so that she was forced to comply or fall out.

Toby, by this time, had got out too, face thunderous as he saw the way Morgan was manhandling Leigh. 'Now just hold on a minute——' he began, only to have his friend turn on him with a snarl.

'No, you wait a minute. Do you think I'm going to stand by and let you get away with this? No chance! You've been asking for this for a long time. Now, by God, you're going to get it!'

Toby rounded the car. 'It will give me the greatest of pleasure to knock some sense into you.'

Leigh stared at them both as if they had gone mad. 'Toby, don't! Morgan, have you lost your mind?'

He didn't take his eyes off his friend as he spoke. 'No. I've made it up at last.'

'Get inside, Leigh, this isn't going to be pretty,' Toby ordered, a grim smile playing about his mouth. 'Any time you're ready, pal.'

'Oh, my God!' They were seriously going to fight and she didn't know how to stop them! Frantically she ransacked her brain for the answer. 'You're both crazy!'

'Not crazy enough to let anyone steal my wife!' Morgan grated. '*My* wife, Toby, not yours or any other man's!'

'Perhaps she is, but you don't deserve her! She's too good for a bastard like you!'

'I know it, but all that's going to change—after I've dealt with you!'

There was another exchange of words, but for the moment Leigh was too stunned to listen. She stared at her husband, seeing his belligerent stance, and realised he was fighting to keep her. For a reason she couldn't fathom, he had thought she was running away with Toby. It was incredible, but not less than the realisation that he was doing it because he loved her.

The knowledge came to her just as the two men closed with each other. She saw Toby duck Morgan's first blow and knew there was no time for dilly-dallying. Only action would do. Behind her lay one of their prized herbaceous borders. With a cry that froze the combatants where they stood, she closed her eyes and sank gracefully into the scented blooms.

CHAPTER ELEVEN

MORGAN reached Leigh first. She recognised his touch on her brow at the same moment she became aware of something sharp digging into her back.

'Leigh?' The anxiety in his voice did her heart good. 'God, what happened?'

'Don't panic,' Toby advised from her other side. 'She's only fainted. You can't leave her lying there. Carry her indoors.'

Bless you, Leigh thought as Morgan hefted her dead weight into his arms. Another second and she would have given the game away. She was going to have more than one bruise, but it was going to be worth it. Her head rested against Morgan's bare shoulder as he carried her into the house and she could hear the frantic thudding of his heart.

Very gently he laid her down on the couch in the lounge. 'I'll get some brandy,' he said, and a second or two later she heard glasses rattling.

When Toby picked up her wrist and felt for her pulse, Leigh very nearly jumped out of her skin.

'Her pulse is OK,' he declared on an odd note as he put her hand down again.

'The brandy's gone. I'll have to get some more,' Morgan said from the other side of the room.

Leigh didn't hear him go out. She waited a second or two, then carefully opened one eye, and found herself staring directly into Toby's speculative eyes as he leant over the back of the couch.

'It's all right, he's gone for the moment,' he told her drily. 'That was a brilliant piece of acting, you even had me fooled!'

Warmth invaded her cheeks. 'If you tell, I'll never speak to you again! Now be a dear and go away.'

Toby didn't budge. 'Not until you tell me what that was all about. It's the second time we've nearly come to blows over you.'

'I will, I will, I promise,' she said quickly, knowing Morgan must be on his way back. 'But not now. Tomorrow.'

'Hmm. I take it everything's all right, then?'

'It is now,' she declared, and her eyes shone. 'Please, Toby...'

'Shush.' His hand came down as a warning and she hastily shut her eyes.

'How is she?' That was Morgan.

'I think she's coming round now,' Toby murmured, and, obedient to command, Leigh groaned.

At once the cushions sank beside her and she opened her eyes to find Morgan sitting watching her, face pale and concerned. 'How do you feel?'

'I'm all right,' she admitted faintly, and tried to sit up.

'Lie still,' he commanded gruffly and she subsided. 'You scared the life out of me.'

'I'm sorry.'

'Well,' Toby said, straightening, 'I think I'd better leave you two alone.'

'Thanks, Toby,' Morgan answered distractedly.

'Given up the idea of taking me apart, have you?'

Morgan did look up then. 'For today. Tomorrow's another matter.'

'Seems to me I'm going to have an interesting day tomorrow. And to think I only came here to tell you I was getting married myself. Whoever said life in the country was dull? Oh, well, have fun, children.' With a wave of his hand, he left them.

Morgan turned from staring at the empty doorway to study Leigh. 'What did he mean?'

This time Leigh sat up. 'He meant what he said. He asked Helen to marry him and she said yes.'

Morgan looked poleaxed. 'Then what the hell was going on this morning?' he demanded tautly.

'Toby was giving me a lift to the church,' she told him softly.

'Church?'

Leigh nodded. 'Yes, church. I wanted to be near Ralph, but my car wouldn't start. Toby arrived and... What did you think was happening, Morgan?' she probed huskily.

Morgan shook his head dazedly. 'The church. I thought——' He stopped abruptly and shot to his feet, pacing over to the window, bracing his hands on the frame and dropping his head. 'I thought you were leaving me.'

Leigh came up on her elbow. 'You thought I was leaving you? That's why you nearly fought Toby?'

The muscles in his back tensed. 'I had to stop you,' he admitted huskily.

'I thought you were going to kill him!'

'I wasn't exactly thinking clearly at the time.'

'But why did you think I was leaving? All my clothes are still here,' she pointed out. 'I didn't even have a case!'

Morgan sighed and lifted his head. 'I told you, I wasn't thinking. I woke up and you weren't in bed. Then I heard a car. When I looked out of the window, you were in Toby's arms. I put two and two together and made five. All I knew was that I had to stop you.'

'Which you did, rather dramatically,' Leigh declared wryly. 'Morgan, this will never do. We can't have our children thinking their father's a hoodlum!'

Morgan swung to face her. 'It's no joke, damn it!' he exploded.

'I know it. Wouldn't it have been easier just to ask me?' she queried gently.

Morgan dragged a hand through his hair. 'Perhaps when I'm old and grey I'll react to you less violently. Right now it seems impossible. My feelings are too strong for moderation.' He sighed revealingly. 'Are you sure you're all right?'

'All I feel at the moment is mystified. Morgan, I told you I was staying,' she reminded him gently. Even at that distance she could see how painful it was for him to swallow.

'I know. But after the way I behaved yesterday, you would have been well within your rights to go. It's what I deserved.' He had trouble getting the words out.

'Well,' she said with a wry smile, 'we don't always get what we deserve.'

'No,' he agreed gruffly. 'You deserved my love and trust, but look what I did.'

Her lids lowered. The time had come for that talk. 'What did you do, Morgan? You said you'd explain.'

He came to her then, and sat down. One hand reached out to tip her chin so that she was looking at him. 'I also said that I loved you. I want you to remember that.'

His eyes were such a clear, sincere blue, they turned her heart over. 'All right.'

For a moment he sat in silence, clearly at a loss how to start. Then he reached for her hand, thumb idly caressing her fingers. 'You'll think I'm a fool.'

'Perhaps I already do.'

He pursed his lips. 'I hurt you.'

'Yes.'

He looked deeply into her eyes and took a deep breath. 'It was that damned will. I was angry at first, especially when I realised what part Una played in its conception. I soon got over being angry at you and Dad. I realised what he had done. I don't suppose he really believed I cared for you. He wanted to protect you. The trouble was, there was nothing to protect me.

'I'd been fighting loving you for so long. I said some very cruel things to you, but nothing made you waver. You still insisted you loved me. Yet still I couldn't admit to how I felt. Then yesterday it all blew up in my face. Suddenly you had the opportunity to be a very wealthy woman. You no longer needed me. I can't remember ever feeling so scared as when that realisation hit me. I knew that there was no reason for you to stay. I had never given you reason. And I'd just made it worse by making that wild accusation. I knew then that I'd destroyed my chances. I couldn't see that anything I had to offer would be enough to make you stay.

'I guess I panicked. I *know* I panicked. I said to myself I had to make you stay any way I could because I couldn't face the thought of your leaving me. That's why I made that stupid attempt to blackmail you. I wasn't thinking too clearly even then, but the inheritance was never the issue. I just used it. What I really thought was that if you had a baby, you'd be certain to stay. I didn't think further than that. I'm sorry if it hurt you, but I just couldn't think of anything else to do. I thought it would work, but it all went wrong.'

Leigh pressed a hand to lips that trembled. 'Didn't it occur to you to simply tell me you loved me?' she queried faintly.

He stared at her blankly. 'I didn't think it would be enough.'

'It would have been more than enough. It would have been everything.'

'Before the will, yes,' he agreed, and there was pain in his eyes as he went on doggedly. 'But could you honestly say the same after it? Can you really say you have no doubts about believing me?'

Leigh didn't look away from the directness of his gaze. 'Yes, I had doubts,' she admitted.

Morgan's shoulders slumped. 'The trust has gone,' he said flatly. 'Not that I blame you. The fault is mine. I'll have to find a way to make you believe me. I want you to trust me. I *need* you to,' he insisted solemnly.

'Morgan, you're not listening. I said I *had* doubts. I don't have them any more.'

'Not even about who I see when I look at you?' he asked squarely.

Leigh swallowed. That was different. 'Who do you see?'

His eyes had never been such a tender blue as they were as he reached out to caress her cheek. 'I see the woman I love. A woman who's passionate and loyal, tender and loving. The only woman I could ever envisage as my wife and the mother of my children. I love you, and I love the child, *our* child, that you're carrying under your heart. I want you to stay, but not with any element of doubt in your heart about my feelings for you. As you so rightly said, the inheritance is mine now, whether you stay or go, because of the baby's existence. I have to wipe out that doubt, so that you'll always know, always be sure, that I love you both and want you both, for who you are.'

Leigh listened with a swelling heart. He loved her, she believed that, totally. She didn't need to have it proved beyond a doubt. It was Morgan who needed to do that, to know he had restored her faith as completely as he could.

'Oh, Morgan, it's not necessary. I can hear the love. I can feel it. There's nothing to prove, ever. Let's put yesterday behind us,' she urged.

He raised her hand to his lips and pressed a kiss to her palm. 'We will, but this is something I have to at least try to do, for myself as much as you.'

Leigh sighed faintly and watched as he closed her fingers about his kiss. He had explained so much, it was only fair she do the same. They were starting their lives from this moment, and, though she hated to raise the subject, she wanted no ghosts to haunt them either.

'Morgan, about Gerald Villiers——' Her words were cut off as a finger was pressed across her lips.

'You don't have to explain anything to me. I trust you, Leigh, completely.'

Her lips brushed his hand with a caress that was mirrored in her eyes as she eased away. 'I know, but I want to explain. I want to be free of the past once and for all.' Her eyes held his, and, with a sigh, he nodded. She took a deep breath. 'Gerald Villiers was a...horrible man, married to a woman I rather liked. It was obvious I wasn't the first woman he'd run after during his marriage, and I could see that Grace suspected it. I didn't want to hurt her, but avoiding him was practically impossible, and he wouldn't take no for an answer. That was when I decided to put an end to his games. I asked for the bracelet for one reason only—so that I could take it straight back to his wife. If you had stayed, you would have witnessed the scene it caused. Both Mother and Gerald were furious, but Grace was the one I cared about. She wrote to me later, after she'd divorced him, thanking me, so I can't regret what I did. I know it looked bad, but I thought you'd understand... eventually.' It was impossible to hide the soft reproach in her voice at the memory.

Morgan swore under his breath. 'Instead I let my anger and distaste override my knowledge of you. What a hell of a mess! I let you down badly, didn't I? What can I say? To say I'm sorry is so damned inadequate, but it's true. That day...' He paused, remembering. 'That day I came home looking forward to seeing you and Dad. Instead, the house was full of Una's friends. Unfortunately for you, when we met in the library I'd just escaped from another of Una's attempts to start an affair. My refusal led to a particularly nasty exchange of words. It left me with a bad taste in my mouth, and in no state of mind to overhear what I did.'

'Which was me apparently seducing Gerald!' she exclaimed in enlightenment.

'Something he didn't deny when I ran into him some months later,' Morgan added grimly. 'I see now it was just a malicious attempt to get at you through me... and it worked. I——'

It was Leigh's turn to cover his lips. 'No,' she commanded, 'I won't have you blaming yourself. We both made mistakes, but it's over now. We're together and we love each other. I just want to forget it all and look to the future, to us. We deserve it, don't we?' she urged huskily.

His smile warmed her heart. 'It's what I want too, and we'll have it just as soon as I keep that promise I made,' he declared in a roughened voice.

Pulling a rueful face, she lay back. 'I suppose you're going to be stubborn about it.'

'So far all I've managed to do is hurt you. This time I want to do something right.'

Leigh reached up a hand to cup his cheek, finding a sensual delight in the slight rasp of stubble beneath her fingers. 'You know it isn't going to work, don't you?' She felt and saw his shock and her lips curved. 'I don't think anything could make me love you more than I already do. There isn't room.'

Morgan closed his eyes, and when he opened them again they reflected rueful amusement. 'Vixen! You did that on purpose.'

She laughed low in her throat. 'Just a small revenge. Do you mind?'

'How can I, when I deserve worse?' Morgan returned wryly. 'Do you feel well enough for me to kiss you?'

'I'm prepared to risk it,' she answered huskily. 'I was beginning to think you'd never ask.'

Morgan lowered his head, eyes warming her with the depth of emotion they revealed. 'I've been a bit slow on the uptake, but I'm learning. It must be because I've had a good teacher.'

Her hands locked about his neck, pulling him down until their lips brushed. 'That was only the beginners' course. It gets better.'

Morgan groaned. 'My God, you pick the damnedest times to seduce me. That faint could have been serious.'

Soon she'd tell him the truth about that, but not now. 'Oh, shut up, Morgan, and kiss me,' Leigh ordered in a passionate whisper, and sighed when he obeyed. His lips were gentle and warm, a feather-light caress that said more in its lack of passion than a thousand passionate kisses ever could.

Slowly Morgan lifted his head, his reluctance plain to see. 'Much as I want to stay here and make love to you, I have to go out.'

'Can't it wait?' she enticed hopefully.

Morgan disengaged her arms and sat up. 'Not this time. What I have to do is important, but it shouldn't take long. That's a promise.'

Leigh sighed. 'In that case, all right, but hurry back.'

He stood up with obvious reluctance. 'I couldn't stay away if you paid me. Take it easy while I'm gone—I don't want you fainting again.'

She flushed guiltily. 'I won't.'

He bent and kissed her swiftly, then left. Feeling happier than she could ever remember, Leigh climbed to her feet and went off to find Rose. Tonight they were going to celebrate and she wanted all their favourite foods. By the time she went up to their room, Morgan had gone. She tidied up after him in a happy daze, then changed into her bikini and went down to the pool to wait for him.

He was gone nearly all the morning, and Leigh was dozing when the sound of his car roused her. Heartbeat accelerating, she picked up the magazine she had been reading and, as soon as she heard his footsteps approaching, pretended to be riveted to it. When his shadow fell on her she glanced up briefly, then down again, and so missed the smile that lit up his eyes from within as he stood looking down at her.

'Interesting story?' he enquired mildly.

'Mm, very,' Leigh agreed.

'It would have to be if you're prepared to read it upside-down,' he remarked silkily.

With a start, she focused on the page before her, and realised it was indeed upside-down. Closing it, she laughed wryly. 'Rats.'

Chuckling, Morgan sat down on the side of the lounger as she made room for him. 'Miss me?' he asked huskily.

'I was asleep,' she replied repressively.

'*Touché.*'

'You were gone a long time,' Leigh pointed out.

'I didn't mean to be, but it took me a long time to find. Apparently there's not much demand for them hereabouts.'

Leigh was totally confused. 'Not much demand for what?'

Blue eyes seemed to impale her as she stared at him. 'Something from the heart,' he said softly.

'Something...Morgan?' Her breathing seemed to be going strangely awry.

From his pocket he produced a small brown paper bag. There was an odd sort of smile on his face when he handed it to her. 'For you.'

There was something about it that made her nerves jangle into life. Her heart was thumping as she unfolded the bag and reached inside. There was only one object there, and she pulled it out, holding it between finger and thumb.

'Why...it's a brass ring,' she said faintly, frowning.

'Not just any ring, darling. Can't you guess? I had to go round half the town to get it. I wanted to give it to you—with all my love.' Morgan's voice carried a husky note of suspense.

He seemed to expect her to know what it was, and suddenly, looking in his eyes, she knew. 'It's a curtain ring!' All at once she was laughing, but there were tears in her eyes. 'Oh, Morgan, you idiot, you remembered.' There was a lump in her throat as she reached for him and was enclosed in his arms.

Morgan pressed his lips into her neck. 'I wanted you to realise just how much I do love you,' he murmured thickly.

Her fingers tangled in his hair, 'Oh, I was wrong. I *can* love you more. I think it will just keep on growing and growing.' She eased away slightly and held out her hand on which the ring lay. 'Put it on,' she urged huskily.

Taking it, Morgan slipped the ring on to join her other rings, then he lifted her hand to his lips and kissed it gently. 'What if it turns your finger green?'

'I'll worry about that if it happens. But don't think you can sit back on your laurels. You may have proved you love me, but I'm the greedy type. I want you to show me, too.'

Gently Morgan brushed his lips over hers. 'I'm never going to stop showing you. That way you'll never have cause to doubt me. I love you, Leigh.'

Beneath his, her lips curved in a smile. 'Show me,' she urged again.

Without further ado, he did.

The door to her past awaited – dare she unlock its secrets?

AVAILABLE IN FEBRUARY. PRICE £3.50

Adopted at sixteen, Julie Malone had no memory of her childhood. Now she discovers that her real identity is Suellen Deveraux – heiress to an enormous family fortune.

She stood to inherit millions, but there were too many unanswered questions – why couldn't she remember her life as Suellen? What had happened to make her flee her home?

As the pieces of the puzzle begin to fall into place, the accidents begin. Strange, eerie events, each more terrifying than the last. Someone is watching and waiting. Someone wants Suellen to disappear forever.

W●RLDWIDE

A
SPECIAL GIFT
FOR
MOTHER'S DAY

Four new Romances by some of your favourite authors
have been selected as a special treat for Mother's Day.

**A CIVILISED
ARRANGEMENT**
Catherine George
THE GEMINI BRIDE
Sally Heywood
**AN IMPOSSIBLE
SITUATION**
Margaret Mayo
LIGHTNING'S LADY
Valerie Parv

Four charming love stories for
only £5.80, the perfect gift for
Mother's Day . . . or you can
even treat yourself.

Look out for the special pack
from January 1991.

Accept 4 Free Romances and 2 Free gifts

• FROM MILLS & BOON •

An irresistible invitation from Mills & Boon Reader Service. Please accept our offer of 4 free romances, a CUDDLY TEDDY and a special MYSTERY GIFT... Then, if you choose, go on to enjoy 6 more exciting Romances every month for just £1.45 each postage and packaging free. Plus our FREE newsletter with author news, competitions and much more.

Send the coupon below at once to:
Reader Service, FREEPOST, P.O. Box 236, Croydon, Surrey CR9 9EL

- - - - — ──── | NO STAMP NEEDED | ── - — - -

YES! Please rush me my 4 Free Romances and 2 FREE Gifts! Please also reserve me a Reader Service Subscription so I can look forward to receiving 6 Brand New Romances each month for just £8.70, post and packing free. If I choose not to subscribe I shall write to you within 10 days. I understand I can keep the free books and gifts whatever I decide. I can cancel or suspend my subscription at any time. I am over 18 years of age.

Name Mr/Mrs/Miss —————————————————— EP86R

Address ——————————————————————————

———————————————————————————————————

———————————————————————— Postcode ——————

Signature ————————————————————————————

Mills & Boon

Next month's Romances

Each month, you can choose from a world of variety in romance with Mills & Boon. These are the new titles to look out for next month.

NO PLACE TOO FAR Robyn Donald

SECOND TIME LOVING Penny Jordan

IRRESISTIBLE ENEMY Lilian Peake

BROKEN DESTINY Sally Wentworth

PAST SECRETS Joanna Mansell

SEED OF VENGEANCE Elizabeth Power

THE TOUCH OF LOVE Vanessa Grant

AN INCONVENIENT MARRIAGE Diana Hamilton

BY DREAMS BETRAYED Sandra Marton

THAT MIDAS MAN Valerie Parv

DESERT INTERLUDE Mons Daveson

LOVE TAKES OVER Lee Stafford

THE JEWELS OF HELEN Jane Donnelly

PROMISE ME TOMORROW Leigh Michaels